AN *ALPHACHAT.COM* NOVEL

VICTORIA ASHLEY & HILARY STORM

Kristiann
♡
Victoria Ashley

Two Can Play
Copyright © 2016 Victoria Ashley & Hilary Storm

Cover Designer:
Dana Leah, Designs by Dana

Cover model:
Dylan Horsh

Photographer:
Furious Fotog

Editor:
Kellie Montgomery

Interior Design & Formatting by:
Christine Borgford, Perfectly Publishable

Chapter
ONE

Blaze

WHAT THE HELL IS THIS crap . . . I put my truck in park as I pull up to the back of the mansion. Nash met me at Rebel's because there was no way I was letting that woman drive home in the state she was in. . She was drunk and devastated that Lynx had walked out on that fucked up mess of a threesome.

I honestly don't know what to think of the whole situation and was surprised when she hit on me to begin with. Watching Lynx's responses to it all didn't give me any more insight either. He was all over the fucking place and I should've known to walk the instant I noticed that. Threesomes have to be *no strings attached* by all three or it is just a disaster waiting to happen.

Any sex between us was never meant to be. Besides that, I'm positive Lynx would've been ready to kill me later just thinking about me touching Rebel. Good thing that shit was diverted. I've been known to get my ass into some serious trouble in the past. I'm hoping to slow some of that down now that I'm trying to really make something of this House and my career.

"Thanks for saving my ass tonight." I finally say something to Nash after a very silent ride home. I've been too lost in my head, trying to figure out what just happened, to talk.

"Look, I don't even want to know what the hell is going on here. Just know, I'll always be a call away to get your ass out of deep shit. Something tells me it won't be the last call I get." I seriously hope it is, but you know shit can change from day to day. Who knows what tomorrow will bring. Hell, we're not even through with tonight yet.

I stare at the side of his cowboy hat and laugh as he assumes probably the worst and speaks what is most likely the truth. "Yeah, probably not." I can't help it. Trouble seems to find me. It can be both a blessing and a curse. He doesn't need to know about the fucked up shit I almost got myself into; besides, something tells me Lynx and Rebel will work it all out and it isn't like me to air other people's dirty laundry.

Jumping out of the truck, I slam my door harder than I expected. Sexual frustration flows over me and I decide I need to find some pussy quick before I get irritated even further. That wouldn't be a fun night for me or our guests.

Shit. I can't believe I almost fucked Rebel. I can't even lie, if Lynx would've been up for it, I would've tore that shit up. She's fine as hell, but honestly, I would've been thinking about a perfect red head that's been torturing my dick ever since she stabbed it three times.

I can't say I don't love the piercings now that I have them, but damn I can't think about my dick without remembering the chaos in my mind as she held it in her hand and sent the most excruciating pain through it. The only good memory from that scene was the feel of her hand around my dick.

Fuck my life, I need pussy now.

I step into the mansion only to see hundreds of women waiting for us to enter. They all move toward me and I can't help but smile that all of these women could be mine if I just said the word. Simple as that. Or complicated as that, depending on which way you look at it.

Moving my eyes around the room, I look for the one that I really want to see, only to be left disappointed when she's not there. Not sure why I even looked for her, this isn't her scene. She's probably at her tattoo shop working like she seems to do so often.

Who else can I take to my room for a quick fuck?

I begin to look at a few of them closer, just trying to choose one quickly. Maybe I need a threesome with two women. Especially since the one earlier was a bust.

I've never felt so awkward in a threesome in my life. I should've known that shit wasn't really going down by the way they both looked at each other. It was obvious she was doing it all out of some sort of revenge and he looked like he was about to kill us all for even thinking it was going to happen.

The last thing I want is Lynx wanting to rip my fucking throat out. That fucker is crazy.

I'm going to have to talk to him about her. He's about to fuck up something there; hell, even I can feel the shit between them. I need to stop thinking about all of that bullshit from earlier and make something happen for myself tonight.

I step back to take in the busy house for just a few seconds until I hear Rome whistle over the railing above me.

"Get the fuck up here. It's time we have a shot."

I follow his lead and move quickly through the mass of women, hands groping me, until I break free from the insanity.

The stairs are easy to get up since they're blocked so that this part of the house is off limits. That's one of the best things we've ever done when it comes to these parties. It's come in handy quite a few times when we need to get away from the chaos down there.

He's still leaning over the railing, looking laid back and chill. His tattoos cover his arms and neck, giving him that bad boy, biker vibe that the women latch onto. "Look at this view. Bodies everywhere. Did you ever think this would be your life?"

My eyes scan the women and I can't stop the smile that forms on my face as I take them in.

"Hell no I didn't, but I'll take this every fuckin' day. This is the shit that could make me one rich fucker." The money I make at the Alpha House is insanity and far more than one guy could even consider spending as fast as it pours in.

I've been working with an investor to do something with all of it until I decide what I want to do with it all. For once in my life I don't want to fuck this up.

"It's fucking beautiful. Which one should I take into my dungeon? I got a new fuck sling I want to try out."

I laugh at Rome knowing what he's talking about. His bedroom is filled with sex furniture. Some of the shit was custom made, and I'm not even sure how he would use it all. I'm sure it wouldn't take much to figure it out with my wild imagination and my experience with sex, but just give me a naked girl and I can make any space work. I don't need any extra equipment to have her screaming my name. I was born with mine.

"I'm sure any in this room would take you up on that offer." I lean forward and look over the railing with him. Half of the girls are watching us and begin to try entirely too hard to impress us. "We should give the girls a show. That's what they're here for." I stand and remove the black neck tie from around my neck and wrap it around both palms, pulling tight and flexing as I do.

The women all turn to watch as I begin to move my hips for a little tease. Rome follows my lead and steps to the side a little and begins to move in his own way and before we have a chance to look down again, the screams fill the entire house. I watch more women come in as we continue our tease.

I rub my cock over my jeans and let them see the bulge reaching all the way across my leg. It's hard not to laugh as they all go insane. This is so much different than having a solo caller to deal with. When I'm doing a show, I have control of the room. Something tells me this room is one dick peek away from complete fucking chaos. Who knows, maybe even a damn riot would break out with some of these crazy bitches. Hell, it's like I'm now living the life of a stripper. A rich fucking stripper, but still like a stripper.

I take the tie and pull it tight between my two hands over the railing, wrapping it tighter around my wrists. They seem to love the idea of me having this tie. I can only imagine all the fun I could have with a sexy ass if I could just find the right one.

It's time to move down the stairs again. I decide to lighten the sexual tension in the room and tie the tie around my forehead. My callers are used to me being goofy. It's part of what makes me the biggest draw in the house. Well, that and my big dick seems to be a help.

I walk slowly down the stairs, over exaggerating my smiles and making eye contact with as many as I can. This is what they all love. They want to see us in character. It's what they all came here to see and who am I to ever hold back pleasing a woman of her desires?

Rome follows me and I catch Knox and Levi circling from the other side. We all make our way to the front and I grab the microphone to torture and tease the women further.

"Tell me ladies . . . did you come here to see us stand around in our fuckin' underwear, or did you come to see us in the flesh?" The screams practically burst my eardrums before I can get all the words out. "Now stay back or Ol' Rambo here will haul your ass out of here. If we pull you up, then you can step up here. If not, stay back and maybe we can work some more of you up here before the night is over."

We had to add security for these parties. It's impossible to work the room and watch it at the same time. Unfortunately we've had to ban some from ever entering the house again. They just don't follow house rules and go all crazy and shit. It's like they have zero boundaries, which I get can happen easily with what we do for them on camera.

The screams get louder at the thought of them having any contact with one of us. I can't even talk yet, because they're still losing their minds at the thought of getting the chance.

It isn't until this very moment that I see Karma finally enter the front door.

Holy. Fuck. This night is about to get real fucking fun if I have anything to say about it.

Chapter TWO

Blaze

THE DRESS SHE'S WEARING SHOWS off some tattoos I've not seen before and my dick instantly twitches at the thought of seeing what else she has underneath the red material that barely covers her gorgeous body. *Fuck.* Her tits are perfect and now my eyes are glued to her every move, not wanting to miss a damn thing. That woman has my undivided attention in a room full of pussy and that is something that never happens.

The sound of Levi clearing his throat reminds me that I'm holding the mic. "MmmHmmm, okay guys, pick your prey, let's get this night started. I already know who I'm going after."

Hands go up all over the room and block my view of Karma. She moves to the far corner and I finally catch her eyes looking toward us. I can see her vibrant red hair hanging over one bare inked up shoulder and before I know it, I can feel myself moving toward her.

Women rub their hands across my chest and stomach as I walk through the crowd, my eyes never leaving her. One even grabs my dick and I just pull her hands from me and keep moving. Karma's not looking at me at all, she's actually looking down at her phone typing something as I approach. Just knowing she has no idea that she's my next victim excites me. The element of surprise should always be in my favor, it's something I love to do. I have to keep them guessing and never let them think they know what to expect from me.

"You came to see me?" My words pull her attention from her phone and I watch her take me in starting at my cock, then slowly moving all the way up to my grinning mouth before she looks at my tie around my head and smiles.

"Who's to say I'm not here for one of the other guys? There are plenty to choose from. I mean, I have been up close and personal with all of you." Her confidence radiates in her tone before she takes one step away from me just as the music begins. Yes, she has been up close to all of us. She's the artist who pierced every single one of the dicks in this house. The guys became insane and decided they like torture and pain and called her to do the honors. She had me stupid from the very moment I looked over the rail and saw her.

On cue, I slide off the tie and hold it tightly in my grip. I move forward on her, pushing her back against the wall and sliding my body over hers before she has time to resist.

I grind my hips forward and raise both of her arms above her head, holding them tightly. Our eyes meet and she exhales against my cheek when I thrust up against her.

Holding both wrists in the grip of my right hand, I let the tie dangle down our arms and continue to stare into her bright blue eyes.

Looking into a woman like this for a long time is something I love to do. There's just something raw about it and I've never met a woman who can stare at me long enough to make me look away first. Call it a challenge at this point, but honestly it tells me so much about a person.

I let my other hand slide down her curves while I continue to watch her. She's looking at me like she's not at all intrigued, even though I can feel that she is.

She wants me. I saw it in the smirk on her face the second I got rough with her.

My cock is literally throbbing as I feel her soft skin under my touch. My hand is full of her ass and I love the challenging look she gives me when I squeeze her once again. "You're gonna love having my cock between your legs."

She raises her eyebrows at me just as I drop the grip on her wrists and slide one of her hands over my erection. She already knows what it looks like from when she pierced it, but that was no comparison to what I'm sporting right now. *I'm completely fucking hard.*

"Nice. A shower and a grower." Her words of appreciation cause me to laugh even though it's not the first time I've heard them.

Fuck yes, I'm hung. How else would I be this successful doing this job? Women love my size and never get tired of watching during a show. Most of them beg for more time.

"I guess I am." I let my lips run over her ear before I continue. "You'll have to give these new piercings a ride and let me know if they're worth the pain I went through."

She squeezes my cock just a little tighter when the sound of Knox's voice echoes through the room. Shit, I want to turn the other way and take Karma to my room and end the teasing right the fuck now.

"You'd like that, wouldn't you?" She smirks again and I can feel a build up of back and forth banter that will lead us both straight into my bed. That's something I'm already expecting, but with more of this teasing, I'll be wound tight, which will only make the sex even more amazing.

"I have a feeling we'd both like that." She continues to squeeze and explore with her touch and it takes everything in me not to slip her hand inside my pants and move this along quickly.

"Alright, Blaze. Bring your catch up here and let's do this." Constant jolts of excitement flow through me as I think of all the fun I'm going to have with this girl tonight. She's in for the fucking ride of her life, because that's what I do.

"I guess I need you to come with me," I breathe against her ear.

Just as I hoped, she smiles and replies with a dirty mind, only making me want her more. "Oh, I'm going to hold you to that coming part."

The smile on my face has to be ridiculous, because holy fuck I want this girl on my dick right the fuck now. I have to finish this party before I haul her up to my room, because I won't be quick with this one.

She follows my lead as I keep a grip on her hand, keeping her close to me. Most of the women make a path for us, and only a few grope me as I pass this time.

She looks a little worried about all of this now, her confidence fading as we move forward in front of a crowd.

"Have a seat." I guide her to the chair, pushing on her shoulders until she's in place directly in front of me. Perfect height for me to really get creative with that mouth of hers, but I'll have to leave that for later.

"Alright boys, it's time to do what we came here to do!" Knox announces loudly and the music starts as the four of us Alpha guys begin moving, our bodies all in sync with each other. I begin to slowly slide my neck tie off my shoulders, just like the others while the crowd loses their minds. I know they can tell where this is headed.

I slip mine around Karma's neck and pull her closer to me,

watching as her breathing picks up. She looks up at me and smiles a naughty fucking grin at me showing me she's ready for whatever I throw her way now that she's up here.

I tie the tie around her and begin to pull just slightly, until she rises to her feet. I let my hands slide down the tie and enjoy brushing over her tits and down her cleavage as I follow the material down. She's biting her lip while I slowly guide her back to her seat, making sure her face is near my chest and stomach all the way down. She's instantly squirming in her seat and I let my fingers trace the edge of both of her tits, no doubt only making the tension worse between the two of us.

Her tits are so damn perfect. They're for sure fake. Now, I know I'm fucking this girl soon. Nothing better than firm titties on a body like she has. I can almost picture them bouncing as she rides my cock while I lie back and enjoy the show.

My fingers leave a trail of chills all the way up her chest until I grab her throat and make her look up at me again.

She looks into my eyes and I can see she's curious. Her eyes show how hungry she is. I like keeping her on the edge of her seat. She's wondering what in the hell I'm going to do next.

I look over at the other guys and see that they've kept up with the moves and I'm the only one faltering. Knowing this just makes me want to scrap this whole fucking routine shit and take her up to my room for the real show I'm craving.

I flip her around until her back is against my chest. Her heart is beating faster and only encouraging me to move forward. I guide her shoulders down until she's bent over in front of me, then I grip the tie in my fist. I tie her hands behind her back with the part of the tie that's hanging low enough to reach. I have to take a step back and look her over because this is something I want embedded into my memory bank. She looks sexy as fuck waiting for me to make a move.

I lean over her and whisper in her ear as I slide the tie around her neck to line it up perfectly. "This is just a tease of what we'll be like together." I pull tight, causing her back to arch and her ass to be in perfect position. She tightens her stance and allows me to grind against her ass.

My cock is begging to make contact with her and I fight the urge to slide her short dress up and do just that. The things I'd do to her sexy ass right here in the open if I didn't want her to myself.

I run my hands over her perfect ass and listen to the sounds of the screams beside me. They're encouraging me to go further, but I'm selfish with her. I don't want to share my time with her with a room full of horny women pretending it's them that I'm touching.

I move my hips against her over and over again. She's making my dick harder by the second and I'm craving so much more from her. I let my hand slide up her side and trace the outside curve of her breast that's not visible to the crowd.

Wanting her even closer to me, I grip her shoulder and pull on the tie even tighter. I slam against her and she grinds against me as I pause any movement and let her move on me. She teases me so perfectly to the point I'm about ready to fuck her right here with everyone watching and say fuck it.

"I'm going to fuck you tonight. I'll have you screaming my name over and over until you can't fucking stand. Then I'll carry you to my bed and fuck you again." She looks over her shoulder at me and curves her lips into the sexiest fucking grin I've ever seen. She's so mischievous and confident, qualities I love in a woman.

She stands still in front of me while I continue to grip the tie and give the audience a show. "Are we just going to sit out here and talk about it, or are you going to fuck me like you say you can?"

She just accepted my challenge and I can't wait to bury myself deep inside her gorgeous body and make her scream for me.

We both stare at each other a little longer with nothing but sexual intensity sparking between us. I don't even notice the crowd moving in closer until I release the grip on the tie and begin to lead her to the stairs.

She pulls the tie from my grip and removes it from her neck. "We're gonna have so much fun with this tie. I'm thinking of all the ways you can tie me up. I have to say Blaze . . . you have me very curious." She pulls her bottom lip between her lips again as she looks over my face slowly. "And that beard. Fuck, I can't wait to feel that right between my legs. I just hope your actions match all that cocky talk I know you're famous for." Her challenge goes right through me.

She stands even closer to me and reaches for my dick again, running her fingers over my piercings and then down over my balls. She holds them both in her hand before she rubs back over my length.

Her moan turns me on even more and I'm now very impatient to get to my room. I fucking love a woman who knows what she wants and isn't afraid to grab it, and fuck if she didn't just grab life by the balls and claim what she wanted.

Once we make it to the stairs, I walk with one hand attempting to hide my hard on. I lead her hand so that she's first to go up and I watch that sexy ass all the way up the stairs while she walks like she knows I'm watching.

Fuck, I'm gonna love fucking that ass.

Chapter
THREE

Blaze

ONCE WE GET TO THE top, I begin to lead her to my room, but she tugs back, stopping me before I can get through the door. "I thought you said you'd fuck me until I can't stand before carrying me to your bed?" She raises a brow, before flashing a sexy grin at me and grabbing the railing. "Are you just all talk or are you the real thing?"

Oh fuck . . . She's perfect for me.

She's a perfect tease and not afraid to speak her mind and go after what she wants.

Closing in behind her, I grip her hips and lift her ass to meet the thickness of my erection, while I lean in to speak next to her ear. "Right here?" I question. "Just because no one is up here to see, doesn't mean they won't be able to hear your screaming over the music as I sink into you."

She grabs my right hand from her hip and lowers it down her body. She moves it between her legs, sliding it up her dress and over the lacy fabric of her panties. The heat from her already wet pussy has my dick about to burst through these damn jeans to get to her. "Prove it."

"Fuck, you asked for it." Adding more pressure to her clit before I pull my hand from between her legs, I begin her undoing. She has no idea how I'm about to make her feel.

I slide my hands around to grip her ass with both hands and slowly lower myself down her body, admiring each and every curve with my mouth on the way. Her skin is soft and her scent is intoxicating and has me inhaling as I move over her.

Placing one hand on her lower back, I push down causing her to arch her back as I place the back of her dress between my teeth. I lift until her ass is on display for me and her red thong stands out against the tattoos on her hips and covers one ass cheek.

Teasing her, I brush my beard along her exposed cheeks and lower her thong down her legs. Her grip on the railing tightens as my hair brushes the soft skin on her legs all the way down and then back up again. I use my tongue sporadically to add even more sensations to her already overloaded skin and listen for every inhale or exhale she makes.

I love the way her perfect little ass pushes out even more, begging for me to touch her with more than just my beard. She wants my dick just as much as I want inside her. Her body says it all.

Smirking, I slap her left ass cheek, making sure to hit close to her pussy lips, but not close enough to touch them. She lets out a small scream, not expecting it, but quickly recovers and bites down before it fully escapes. She follows up with a frustrated grumble before she speaks. "You're a tease too I see. This ought to be fun." She breathes out like she's forcing herself to be patient. I get it, it's exactly how I feel.

I make my way back up her body, my hands roaming on the way up. I lean in to whisper in her ear for the second time. Mostly because I know my deep voice works women up. "I'm a lot of things. Your sexy ass will find out soon enough just how much of a tease I can truly be."

Turning her face, I capture her lips with mine, but she bites me and laughs against my lips. "I never said you could kiss me."

"Yet you want me to fuck you?" I point out, knowing this isn't unusual, but is always weird to me. If my dick is good enough for you, so is my fucking tongue.

She bites my bottom lip again and tugs on it before releasing it. "A woman has needs just like a man does. Doesn't mean I want anything more. I don't do this often, so don't give me reasons to stop tonight."

Hearing her say that she doesn't do this often only makes my body crave her even more. Turning her face away, I give her payback and bite her neck while I slide my finger down her ass and between her wet slit.

I slowly slide a finger inside her, taking in every moan and squirm her body makes. Her tightness makes me believe that it's been months since anyone's been inside of her. This shouldn't make me as happy as it does, but it's now consuming me.

She moans, while reaching around with one hand and finding the zipper of my pants, tugging until I'm exposed.

I begin to slide my finger in and out of her tight little pussy faster, while she works my pants over my hips. She stops once she has them halfway down my right hip and her fingers graze my 'V' muscle, before lowering to my thong and snapping the strap.

"You boys really know how to work a crowd of horny women up. I never thought a man-thong could be so damn sexy."

She snaps the strap again with a grin. So I lift her further over the railing and slip another finger inside of her, going in deep.

She's on the tips of her toes in her heels now and I know she has a good view of the floor below us.

From the way her breathing picks up again, she loves it rough and dangerous. And fuck if I'm not the one that can give her just that.

"Hold on tight," I bite out, before slapping her ass again. Holding a firm grip, I squeeze a tight grip and kick out of my shoes.

With my free hand, I reach for the condom in my pocket and rip the wrapper open with my teeth. My pants fall to my feet so I can kick out of them too. Then I lose this uncomfortable as fuck thong and kick it all out of my way.

I'm standing here completely naked now with just the tie resting around my shoulders and the girl of my dreams bent over in front of me waiting for me to take her. I couldn't ask for a better scenario than right now.

I'm impatient as fuck now and all I want to do is bury my cock inside Karma and let her feel the work she did on me.

While sliding the condom on with one hand, I slide the top of her dress down her shoulders with the other, until her breasts are exposed for my touching.

I want to feel her tits in my hands as I fuck her, but I don't want any of the assholes who might walk by below seeing them. Just the thought of that pisses me off.

I run my hands over her breasts, admiring them, before cupping them both, doing my best to keep them covered. Her piercings rub over my fingers and make me want to see her tits closer.

"Fuck, you're the perfect size." I make sure that my cock is lined up with her entrance before pushing forward against her. "Your pussy might be another story. Prepare yourself."

Getting a firm grip on her breasts, I slide inside, stopping once I'm in as far as I can go. I'm not all the way in, but rarely do I get to go balls deep during a first time with someone.

She squeezes my hand and bites into my arm as if preparing for my intrusion. "Don't stop. Oh shit."

We both moan out as I let her adjust to me while I slide in and out of her slowly three times, before pulling out and slamming back into her. *Fuckkkk me.*

There's no way I can hold back any longer with this woman. She feels too fucking good.

"Oh shit!" she screams out again, before biting even harder on my arm as I pull out and slam back inside her once again. Her response only causes me to go harder and deeper with each thrust.

I pull her body back against mine until there's no space between us. I don't want anything separating my skin from hers. I just want her to feel what I can give her. I want this fast and hard so I can get her where I want her, in my room, in my bed taking me in every way possible.

Wrapping one arm around her breasts and the other around her neck, I hold on tightly as I slam into her, over and over again until it feels as if her legs are giving out on her. I've never fucked so hard and fast in my life. I'll admit it, she brings out an entirely new level of desperation inside of my chest.

I can feel her grip on me tightening as if she's using me for support. I lift her legs and hold them around my waist as I continue to fuck her through an orgasm. She's still moaning when the door below opens.

We both look below when Knox walks into view. "Holy fuck man. You get all the good ones." His whistle and comments as he keeps walking make me smile. I won't argue with that. In fact, I'll agree with him.

I only slow down to let her get a better grip, but quickly notice she's no longer steady on her feet. Good . . . now I can take her to my bed and really show her what I can do.

Pulling out of her, I keep my hands on her to keep her from falling and turn her around to face me. "Point proven." She looks fucked and I've only just begun. I raise a brow as she comments because I know she thinks it's over.

"Now the fun begins." I grab her thighs and pick her up, sliding back into her as she wraps her legs around my waist. She holds me as I begin to walk and fuck her at the same time. She looks sexy bouncing up and down on my cock.

My room couldn't be any further away right fucking now. It might just be down the hall, but anywhere but right here is too far at the moment.

Pushing the door to my room open, I walk toward my bed, tossing her down as soon as we get close enough.

She keeps reacting to anything rough so I'm going to continue to give it to her hard. Plus, there's no way I can make it gentle now even if I tried. Especially with the way she's looking on my bed. So fucking perfect and just as hungry as I am.

Looking up at me from the bed, she looks impressed, but tries hard to hide it. It's as if she doesn't want me to know how much she's enjoying it, but she can't hide that shit from me. I specialize in picking up on what a woman wants.

Crawling above her, I grip both of her hands and slide her up the bed until she's at the headboard.

Then I pull the tie from my neck and bind her hands above her head to one of the bars. It's just loose enough for me to flip her over and position her any way I want.

She leans on the pillow and buries her face when I give her ass a slap and slide back inside of her. Now I can play. I can take all fucking night doing this right here.

I move in slowly inside her, gripping her rounded ass as I do. She has so much ink across her back and I can't even let myself focus on what she has exactly. My cock is clouding my care at the moment.

Could she feel any better on my dick? I slam into her as deep as I can and grip her long, red hair, wrapping it up in my hand as I pull back.

"Damn . . . those piercings," she says out of breath. "So. Fucking. Good. I'm about to come harder than I ever have. Please don't stop."

I pull her hair back, until my lips are pressed against her ear. "I won't, baby."

"Ohhhh. Fuck me Blaze. Quit teasing me and show me what you can do. Show me you're not all talk." She's so needy with her demand and I take it as success. She's another one that'll be dick crazy once I'm finished with her, if she isn't already.

"I love a challenge. You'll be screaming my name and begging me to let you sleep before I'm finished."

"That's what I'm counting on," she says with a slight laugh. "The guys I know are quitters. They can't handle a woman that loves sex and needs an orgasm."

I pull out and slam back into her, moaning as I do. "I can," I say firmly. "Hope you can handle a man that can give it to you. 'Cause there's no way you're only coming once with me."

Before she can respond, I reach around and rub her clit with my free hand, while fucking her hard and fast, until she's screaming out and her pussy is clenching my cock. She's coming on my fingers before I finish and her body begins to quiver and shake while she comes down from her high.

I barely give her time to recover before I untie her from the bed and flip us over so that she's riding my face.

She looks down at me and grips my hair, while still trembling above me, her pussy still sensitive and her lips shivering with satisfaction. "But you haven't . . ."

"Oh I will. Trust me. Right now I have something to prove."

I grip her hips and run my tongue over her swollen clit, making her squirm above me. "Pull my hair if you have to, but don't stop riding my face until I taste your next release on my tongue."

Spreading her legs further apart, I gently blow on her pussy, before running the tip of my tongue from her opening, up to her clit.

Placing my mouth around it, I flick my tongue up and down before moving it in a circular motion to work her up more.

Once she's grinding her hips onto me as if she's about to lose it, I shove my tongue into her pussy and fuck her with my tongue.

This has her riding my face so hard that I can barely breathe.

"Oh my god. Yes!" She grips my hair harder and yanks it hard, never stopping her determined pace of riding my face. "I'm about to . . ."

I place my thumb over her clit and relentlessly rub circles when I feel her about to lose it above me. I watch her tits move as she does and damn if they aren't just as perfect as I thought they'd be. The piercings only tease me further.

"Holy fuck!" she screams out, while squeezing my face with her thighs as she comes for the third time in five minutes. "I can't breathe . . . so good. It feels so . . ."

As she fights to catch her breath, I flip her over on her back and slide back into her, causing her to slap my shoulder and squeeze it.

"It's sensitive, holy shit . . ."

I smirk down at her. "Isn't that what you wanted?"

She doesn't respond as I begin to grind my hips, being slow and gentle at first. She just closes her eyes and digs her nails into my back.

"I need to work on my endurance. It's your turn," she whispers. She's already exhausted and I get it. I'm a little overwhelming when it comes to sex.

Gripping her thighs and pushing them back, I thrust my hips and pound into her until I feel my release building. I have to pull out quick so I place her hand around my cock and let her know that I want her to jerk me until she finishes me off. She grips me tight and it's not hardly any effort on her part to take me home.

I'm extra careful about releasing myself inside a woman, even with a condom. I've yet to do it.

We both lay back on my bed, while fighting to catch our breath. Neither of us speak. The moment is just too perfect for words.

After about five minutes of silence, Karma stands from my bed and starts fixing her clothes.

"I guess I should admit that you proved me wrong."

"Yeah . . ." I smile up at her. "Tell me how."

"Not *every* man I know is a quitter and some actually know how to please a woman." She turns to walk toward the door. "Maybe I'll see you around."

I sit up, realizing that she's running on me. "Or I could call you," I suggest, even though I never do this shit. Usually I'm looking for ways to get them to leave at this point.

"I don't give my number out to men. It's sort of a rule of mine."

My heart is racing because even though I've already had her, I'm not ready for her to walk away from me. "Then I'll give you mine."

She raises a brow and pulls the door open with confidence and a no-nonsense glare telling me my answer before she even opens up her mouth. "No, thank you. If we see each other then we see each other." She smiles at me and blows me a kiss. "Bye, Blaze."

I release a breath and run my hands through my sweaty hair

and down my face as the door closes behind her.

She just pulled the fuck and run on me and fuck me, if I don't want her more now . . .

Chapter FOUR

Karma

I FEEL THOROUGHLY FUCKED, YET I want to walk back through that door and sit right back on his face.

I could tell he was going to have me screaming just by the look in his eyes the first time I met him. Piercing him was quite the pleasure, but it was nothing like fucking him.

Who knows, one day maybe we'll hook up again, but until then I need to get my ass to the shop. I hope I still have clients waiting on me at this point. I'm much later than I expected.

I look down at my phone and see multiple text messages from Charlie at the shop. She knew I'd be a little late tonight, but I'm now almost two hours late and that isn't like me at all. She's freaking out at this point and I don't blame her.

I shoot her a text telling her I'm on my way, before I race down the stairs and out the door of the mansion.

Fuck and forget. That's what I do when I actually let myself hook up with anyone. After all, it's what men do, so I may as well beat them to it.

Lately, I haven't had the patience to deal with men and their bullshit. Running my shop has been my main focus, and needs to remain that way, until I'm able to add that extra shop in California like I've always wanted to do.

I started out just doing tattoos, but more recently have added piercing, to keep my clients coming back for multiple reasons.

I actually enjoy tattooing more, but piercing is quick and easy money. When I got the call to come to the house to pierce all of the guys in the Alpha house, it was a no brainer for me to get in on that kind of promotion.

Since the pictures went live, my shop has been out of control and I can't seem to get enough talent in to take care of all of the demands, which is the exact reason why I should be there on the busiest night of the week.

I should've known it'd turn into a longer stop than I expected. His body alone was reason enough to make me stay longer than planned. That doesn't even cover what he can do with that body.

My phone begins to ring just as I slide into the driver's seat of my car.

"Damn, woman. I was just about to send the guys out to find your ass on the side of the road." Charlie's laughter fills the phone. "Did ya get lost?"

"I'm five minutes out," I explain, hoping she'll refrain from asking questions. "Just tell my clients I'll stay until everyone gets what they came for." I start the engine and hope like hell she'll leave it at that.

"Can you at least tell me you have one fucking damn good reason for disappearing like this? This isn't like you at all, Karma."

She's my shop manager and for that reason I have to keep her informed, but fucking Blaze is one thing I'll never share with her.

"I had to make a stop and it took longer than I thought. I'll be there in just a minute. Get my first client registered and then keep them coming. It's mostly piercings tonight anyway so it should go quickly."

"You know I'm taking care of things in here. I've been entertaining them and selling the shit out of the jewelry they'll all need to change up the look. One guy is taking a time slot at the end of your shift, just to free some time up. We'll be good until you arrive."

"What guy is that?"

"His name is Ryan."

My breath halts instantly. He wouldn't dare come to my shop and start shit, would he? Hell, I'm not even sure it's *the* Ryan I should be worried about, but just hearing his name sends me into a cluster of emotions I don't want to deal with.

"Charlie, I'm almost there. I'll see you in just a second." I hang up and try to regain my professional appearance before I walk into a shop full of eyes on me for being late.

I look fucked. *I feel fucked.* And I just hope that before this night is over, I'm not fucked dealing with the Ryan I used to know.

Pulling up to the shop, I decide to park in the front tonight. I wish I could shake this uneasy feeling that one of the biggest assholes from my past is about to walk through my doors and try to manipulate his way into my life again.

He has never taken me saying no very well, we established that many times in the past.

I fix my makeup quickly before I step out of the car, my heart racing from the tension I now feel.

My artists know I never step through those doors looking less than perfect, but this might have to be a first for me. One quick glance back at my reflection in the windows and I see that my hair is a mess, so I quickly reach in for a clip and pull it up. I slide back in my car and strip out of my fancy dress and tone it down by putting on a more comfortable one. There's no way I can wear that fancy shit and work.

One last look doesn't really make me feel any better. It's not my best, but it'll have to do.

This night has been pure fucking chaos. I need to remember how this rushed feeling is the next time I decide to stop in at the Alpha house, even if my intentions were only to see what one of their parties was like.

I can see why they're as successful as they are. Hell, the women there were ridiculous and I need to consider getting in on the next party they have. I could bring in my artists and offer work on any of the guests that show up. Maybe Lynx and I can work out some special in house rates for his clients, which will just increase business even more for my shop.

Fuck, I need to get more help in here.

Charlie is the first person I see when I walk into the shop. She's standing there, twirling her pink hair around her finger and chewing her usual gum, while looking at the computer.

"Charlie, remind me to put out another ad for artists. We're going to need to get more in here quick. I've been brainstorming." She looks at me with a huge smile on her face, welcoming the information to grow the shop even further.

"Sure thing, boss lady. We could definitely use some more men in this place." I knew she'd welcome that idea. She's been asking for more eye candy in the shop for months now. She said it helps her day go by faster. I can't even argue with her on that.

"Also, let me see the paperwork on my last client of the night." I need to see if he really has the balls to come to me again.

"He didn't fill out the paperwork yet, said he'd come a few minutes early to get it done."

Fucking great . . .

"What did he look like?" I question. I need to get to the

bottom of this so I can let it go and get my work done.

She looks up from the counter. "He's got a shit ton of tattoos, like almost as many as Bones."

I close my eyes knowing it's him. *Damn it.* Bones is one of my artists and is very tattooed. Ryan is a tattoo artist as well and has ink up his neck and all the way down both of his hands.

My heart begins to beat fast just thinking about him. What could he possibly want from me after everything we've been through?

I take a look at the people waiting on me when the shop phone rings, interrupting us. A small understanding smile from each of them lets me know they're not too pissed off at me, so now I just need to get my shit together and move forward on this night so I can still get to each of them.

"Boss. There's a man that says he'll pay ten grand to get a session this week. I told him you were booked out three months and he told me to fuck off with that." She's laughing as she continues and I look at her like she's crazy. "Sounds like he really wants you."

Can this night get any weirder?

"What? Who is it?" I watch her hit mute on the receiver and look at me with a giant smile.

"He said you've screamed his name a few times tonight."

Holy shit. That fucker.

My face flushes instantly and I consider slamming the phone down, as she hands it to me, with the most ridiculous look on her face. It's like she's proud that I finally got laid or something. It's not like it's been that damn long. But with her, even two days without sex is too long.

"I'm booked for months. Your money doesn't change that." I don't even say hello or give him the chance to say anything before I speak sternly into the phone. I can't believe he even called my shop with such a ridiculous fucking request. He's so cocky that I want to strangle him through this phone.

His confident laughter frustrates me even further. "You could just give me a private session after hours, that's what I really want anyway. You can tattoo me while we're both naked."

"I'm busy. I have clients lined up and don't have time to deal with you tonight." I try to dismiss him quickly, but I should've known he'd be more difficult than that.

"Make time." His confidence is obvious in the way he speaks, and I admit that I find that extremely sexy.

"I can't."

"What time is your last client tonight then, I'll just come there to get it sketched out or something."

He just will not quit.

My mind goes to Ryan and the dread I feel that he'll be coming in. Maybe it won't be such a bad idea to have someone lined up right after him, even if it means I'll be working extremely late into the night. Anything to get Ryan pushed out that door as quickly as possible sounds like a good option.

"My last client arrives at midnight. Get here before then to fill out the paperwork and we'll talk once I'm finished with him. Don't be late." He begins to talk and I just hand the phone to Charlie.

I don't have time for anymore of the shit that seems to be at a constant downpour on me tonight.

Releasing a breath, I walk into my private room and find two females sitting there waiting patiently. I look at their chart and see that I'm doing nipple piercings on both of them.

Hitting the music, I wash up and finally get my night started. "Alright, tops off so we can get you marked properly." They both smile and don't hesitate to strip out of their tank tops and bras. I start to mark the first one before they begin to talk.

I don't really catch much of what they say, until a certain name comes up, catching my attention.

"I bet Blaze will love your tits even more now." The blonde looks down with a grin on her face before she responds with excitement.

"I know he will. I can't wait to show him. I just hope the pain will be worth the pleasure that will eventually come with having these." What are the odds that this is the same Blaze? *And why do I care if it is?*

"My next call with him is tomorrow night."

There it is. It sure as hell is the Blaze I know. I keep quiet and just do my job perfectly as usual. Their stories won't distract me into messing these up.

"I don't care about your next call with him, when will he be over again? I could use another night with that friend of his." I finish piercing the blonde before I clean up and start on the brunette.

Knowing about Blaze before I went there tonight, I knew he was experienced and there would be numerous women out there that know him intimately. I just wasn't ready for them to be in my face so quickly. Not that it matters, but shit if this doesn't make me feel like he's the perfect one to use for sex when I need it. He can't get too attached with that kind of reputation.

I seem to only be attracted to men like him. It's easy to fuck and move on, they don't truly want anything more than that anyway. I knew this going in to his room tonight and that's the exact reason I will only ever be a fuck buddy at best with him.

I don't have to like these bitches though. Outside of being my clients, I don't owe them anything beyond that. I can feel my bitch face taking over quickly, so I turn to make the notes I need to once I finish. "Take a look and tell me what you think." I point to the mirror and they both stand side by side in front of it.

"We should send him a picture right now." The blonde grabs her phone and they both pose. I stand purposely out of the view and wait impatiently as they continue to make me crazy.

"Who knows, maybe we should take him up on that three-some thing after this. Your tits look amazing and I know he has a thing for pierced nipples." They both begin to laugh and agree how amazing that would be.

"I bet he can handle both of us without any issues. That man definitely has a lot of stamina and I'm hoping to find out what he would do with both of us."

Fuck my life, this is what I get for going for the one with the biggest dick.

Chapter FIVE

Blaze

I NEED TO GET THE hell out of here. "I have somewhere important to be, Lynx. I know you've had a shitty night with Rebel, but I have an appointment."

I step around his angry ass as he stares me down and start down the back stairs to leave without being noticed by the crowd.

He doesn't stop me and I'm thankful. Karma is fucking with my mind and I'm going to get a piece of her again, because that little show wasn't nearly enough for me to say that I've scratched that itch. *I fucking need more of her.*

I take my truck to her shop and notice there are only four cars and a motorcycle in the parking lot. It's after midnight, but only by a few minutes.

The sign says closed, but I go to the door anyway, knowing that she's expecting me. A girl with pink and blue hair greets me and locks the door behind me.

"You here for Karma?" I nod at her and try not to watch her legs in that short ass skirt as she bends over to fix a rug. Any one of the other guys in the house would jump at a chance to fuck her, but all I can think about is getting to Karma. "She's got one more piercing to finish, then you're up."

I walk around the front of the shop, taking in all the pictures of finished tattoos. I catch her signature at the bottom of one, then go back over them, taking note of all of hers specifically. She's a very talented artist, which only makes me more excited to get an even larger tattoo than I planned.

Before I can finish looking at all of the proof of her talents, the music stops overhead and her voice echoes in my ears, instantly causing me to be on guard.

She's angry and I can't make out every word she's saying, but I hear a few words before the door opens. She's trying to get someone to leave and they don't seem to get the fucking hint.

"I'm finished. I have work to do so Ryan, please go." Her small body is no comparison to his large physique and I find myself instantly watching his reaction to her demands. He's not moving toward the door and it heats me up very quickly.

I take a few steps toward her door before she looks over at me and then back to this Ryan fucker. "Please go. I'll call the fucking police to get your ass out if I have to." He finally stands only to step toward her and close the door once again.

Before I even acknowledge what I'm doing, I'm in the room with them, I've slammed him against the wall and my arm is held tight against his throat. "She said to leave, mother fucker. What do you not understand?"

His wicked grin shows me how fucked up he is and how bad shit is about to get if he decides to fight against me. I don't want to fuck up her entire shop, but I will just to see this trash taken out.

I can feel the veins in my forehead bulging as I think about fucking this guy up. I press harder and grip him to start dragging him to the front door.

"Stop. I can handle my own shit, Blaze." Her anger is felt in the room and I can't tell if I've overreacted to this situation, or if she's just downplaying it all trying to be Miss Independent on my ass and not need a damn man.

"I'm leaving . . . for now. But I'll be back, Karma. Don't think for one fucking second that I won't. You know me better than that. We have a lot of fucking history and that shit doesn't just go away."

His dark eyes focus on her when I back away. I remain in between the two of them, ready to tear his ass up if he takes one step toward her.

"I'll always be near and watching. Just remember that." His threat confirms to me that I didn't overreact and she needs to let me take care of this piece of shit.

"Don't threaten her again. I'm giving you one last chance to leave on your own before I throw your ass out of here."

His fucked up laughter irritates me and is the final straw that causes me to snap. I slam him into the wall again and get in his face, holding back the urge to fight him all the way out the door. "How about you and I step outside for a little one on one chat about how this is all going to go?"

He pushes against me, trying to get me to move, but I don't budge. Fuck that shit. "Pretty boy, I'd murder you. Get the fuck off of me. I'm going."

We stare at each other for a few seconds before I back off. I can tell he'll be back for her and that makes me even crazier thinking about that. She just happened to get lucky that I was here tonight to stop him. Next time she might not be so damn lucky.

I take a few steps back and allow him the space to walk out, but not to get close to her again. He turns before he walks out the door, grabs his cock and begins to speak. "Thanks again, Karma. As usual, you were sexy as fuck and felt perfect around my cock. You were made for me. Remember that. It'll always be me and you." He smirks, then walks out the shop before the pink haired girl locks it once again.

Karma releases a deep breath, like she's been holding it for minutes, then she begins pacing.

"Who was that?" I have to ask questions because I hate how my gut is telling me he'll be back.

"My ex." She opens a drawer and puts a small pistol in a box, before she turns to look at me. I had no idea she was holding that gun.

"Karma."

"Just don't." She stops me instantly, not allowing me to continue. She's pissed and I can feel it all around me. "We fucked once. That doesn't give you any say when it comes to my life." She's anxious and won't even look at me as she starts to spout off her bullshit.

"Us fucking has nothing to do with my logic. Has he hurt you in the past?" She stops moving, only verifying my instincts.

My blood boils at the thought of his hands on her, hurting her in any way. Only filth would hit a woman and I can tell he's one filthy fucker.

"You need some damn security in here if you'll be working this late by your damn self," I say firmly. "Even if I have to come here personally and do it myself."

"I have people here. Plus, I'm armed and will have more artists soon. He can't really hurt me anymore, so I'm not worried about him."

"So is that why you had a gun in your hand? How exactly did you plan on getting him off of you? Shooting him while he towers over your small body?"

She finally looks into my eyes before she responds. Her blue eyes pierce mine with intensity. "Blaze, drop it. I can handle him.

Thank you for stepping in tonight, but don't ever do that shit again. Got it?"

I stand silently, staring into her eyes all the while making a few plans of my own to make sure she's not alone this late at night again.

"Can I work you in another night? My mind is a mess and I want to be able to give you the best I can, and right now that's not possible." She looks at me with a sadness in her eyes that I hate right away.

I don't know what her past is with this guy, but it clearly was not a good situation and my imagination is definitely giving me plenty of scenarios of how it went down.

It only makes me want to kill him myself so she never has to deal with him again.

"I'll let you work the tattoo later, but I'm not leaving." She relaxes after I reply and that gives me one ounce of hope that she's actually going to spend some real time with me.

"You know I didn't fuck him, right? I pierced his dick. He was just saying all of that to get a rise out of me." She explains herself even though she doesn't have to, but I have to say, relief washes over me to know he didn't get to touch her when I'm still on her skin from earlier.

"That doesn't surprise me." I step closer, backing her against the same wall I just had him pinned against.

"Boss. Do you need me to stay late?" The pink haired girl pushes the door open wider and I don't move a muscle.

Karma's eyes don't leave mine and we both breathe against each other's face. I can feel my cock twitching between us even though I'm trying to hold back.

"Thanks, Charlie. I think I can handle it from here. Is Bones still here?"

"He's finishing up now. I'll lock up and leave with him, if

you think it's ok to do so?"

My cock decides to tell me to fuck off and gets excited at the fact that we're about to be alone again. There's no hiding the fact that I want inside her again.

She nods at Charlie and I smile like I just won the damn lottery.

I'm getting ready to give her the fucking of her life, especially now that my adrenaline is pumping full of rage that didn't get released.

Chapter SIX

Karma

MY EMOTIONS ARE ALL OVER the place tonight. I was hoping I'd never see Ryan again, but I should've known I wouldn't be that damn lucky.

He's an insensitive ass and it breaks my heart that I let him be in my life for as long as I did. The things he's done to me can never be forgiven. I honestly can't believe I agreed to pierce him tonight.

He was adamant that I be the one to do that for him since he taught me everything I know. After I had his dick in my hands, he changed his entire demeanor and then started talking about missing my touch.

It took everything I had not to truly stab him in his hard dick, but I held back knowing he would be gone soon, one way or another.

I definitely found comfort in knowing Blaze would be here tonight. That feeling both soothed me and pissed me off. I don't want to become dependent on another man, in fact I never will again. I'll make damn sure of that.

"You should come home with me." Blaze is pressed up

against me, his hands running down my body, tempting me in all the perfect ways, but I have no desire to go home with him. His house is full of insanity and that's something I've had enough of tonight.

"That's the last thing I should do." My response is breathy and almost pathetic. He has a way of making me feel so good and now my body betrays my intentions with him by craving more.

"I could convince you otherwise," he breathes. His hand reaches between my legs as he slides his fingers under my panties, touching me so damn good. His other hand raises my dress and lifts my ass until I'm pulled up against him.

Damn him for being this demanding and damn me for loving it.

"Your place is crazy tonight. Maybe some other night."

He smiles like he knows he just won, with my weakness of the promise of great sex. I have to admit, he's hands down the best I've had and I know we just barely touched the surface of the possibilities between us.

"Ok then, we'll go to your place." He speaks with his lips brushing over my cheek and his fingers dipping further inside me. He's so damn hard to resist right now.

I moan some sort of response that neither agrees nor denies him. I hear Charlie yell out that they're leaving and that only sends desperate intensity between Blaze's body and mine.

He moves his fingers faster in and out of me before he leaves me empty and wraps my legs around his waist.

"Or we could just fuck right here." He's walking me to the table that I lay my clients on before I stop him.

"No. We'll go to my place. Just give me a minute and you can follow me there." I'm in the mood for a little more than just a quick fuck that we had earlier and I hope he is too. The stress of tonight needs to just fade away and this seems like the perfect distraction.

"I'm getting your fucking number after this." He sets me down and watches me closely. His hand slides around the back of my neck and into my hair, sending a chill over my body and making me want him to continue.

"Why do you pretend to want my number? We both know you'll never use it." His look changes as his eyes focus on mine again like he's trying to figure me out.

"Oh, I have a feeling I'll be calling you often, but we can talk about all of this later because I'm giving you a five-minute warning before I fuck you right here. You have my dick bulging at the thought of fucking you again. Time starts now."

He steps back and watches me move around the shop, shutting the last of it all down. Thanks to Charlie, there's not much left to do, so I pull the money bag from the drawer and we both head to the door.

He follows me closely as I drive less than a few miles to my house. I watch the headlights from his truck in the rear view mirror and catch myself in disbelief over what I'm about to do again.

I've gone months without sex just to stay focused on building my business up here and in one day he has me coming back for more, practically craving his touch.

I park in the garage and he meets me before I can even get out of the car. He reaches for my hand and holds it as if he's assisting me out of the car, only to pull me into his chest once I'm standing.

"Your five minutes are up." His deep voice bolts through my body and promises pleasure in simply the tone of his voice.

"Can I at least close the garage door? Or should we just fuck in my driveway for all the neighbors to see?" He smiles at my reply and leans in until our lips are connected, teasing me with his tongue and forcing my back against the side of my car.

"Your choice. You know I'm down for people watching." He moves quickly, allowing his hands to slide over my body until he's touched me everywhere it counts again.

"Karma. How are you this fucking sexy? You have me dying to see all of your tattoos again, since my impatient ass didn't pay attention last time."

He begins to kiss down my neck and chest, sending a tingling rush over my skin. He slides the material of my dress down exposing my breasts, taking in one nipple before the other, biting just slightly on the metal in each one.

My mind goes back to the girls in my shop tonight. "So I hear you really like nipple piercings." He mumbles something as he pushes both of my tits together and buries his face, licking his way around them both.

"Fuck yes I do." His touch feels so good, I decide to drop any comments I want to make and just let him do his magic. "Let's go inside."

"I was looking forward to the neighbors knowing my name." His cocky grin has me laughing when he wraps my legs around his waist again, picking me up and walking me inside. "But I guess they'll still hear you from inside. Hit the button when we pass and tell me where I'm going." He's so damn demanding and I can't even stop him because he's matching what I want.

I let him carry me and kiss me all the way inside. His hands move under my dress before he grips my panties, yanking them with enough force to rip them. I shift my hips and the lace falls to the floor just inside the kitchen.

He walks me to the nearest wall before he rests me against it and pulls his shirt over his head.

Shit, his shoulders seem even larger with his shirt off. I can't stop myself from running my hands over him. The bulging muscles make it a rough pass over his shoulders and arms and I find that sexy as hell. I can't get enough of his body.

"Alright, I'm about to fuck you in every room of this house since you seem to be at a loss of words. How do you feel about the kitchen table?"

He takes my breath away as he rolls his hips forward, rubbing his bulging jeans over my clit and biting my lip at the same time. His large hands pull me even closer against him while his tongue begins to leave a wet trail down my neck.

In an instant, he has consumed me.

"I don't care where, Blaze. Just fuck me." I grow greedy and impatient the more he moves on me, working me up yet again.

"How do I get out the back door?" He speaks between rough kisses and heavy breathing, desperate to get where we're going.

"Behind you." He grips my ass and begins to walk us both outside. I wrap my arms around his neck and bite his shoulder, before I rake my nails across his back, no doubt leaving marks as I do.

"Fucking hell. That's it. Since you seem to like it rough, that's what you're getting again."

I don't have time to respond before my back is against the brick wall and he's ripping my dress from my chest. The moon shines brightly on us as I look into his eyes, watching his every move.

The aggression in his touch turns me on more than ever and I can barely handle waiting for him to free his cock and put a condom on.

Our breathing is loud already, but gets louder as he enters me. He feels so good as he works his way deeper with each thrust.

My back scrapes against the rough bricks each time he moves us, my dress blocking part of it, but my shoulders bearing the most.

"Fuck, you feel so good." He moves into me hard, exhaling against my cheek as he does. He flattens his hands out on the wall beside my head on both sides and I wrap myself tighter around his body.

He keeps moving us until I'm rotating my hips and thrusting myself up and down his cock, screaming through an orgasm. I don't care at the moment who can hear me, I want to see this orgasm through to the very end. I keep moving on him until I'm literally dripping wet from my own release.

The rush of the moment leaves me breathless and sensitive to his next thrust. I pull back and he knows to enter me slowly this time. The smile on his face as he moves forward to kiss me tells me he's proud of himself for sending me into that crazy spin of chaos. And this time I let him kiss me without resisting.

I'll let him have that moment of accomplishment, because he literally made me climb him and ride him like I've never been fucked before in my life.

His cock makes me crazy and it's going to be hell getting him out of my mind after this day.

Chapter SEVEN

Blaze

I'M NOT GOING TO LIE, every call that I've had this damn week, I've been imagining Karma's perfect body and how good it felt to be buried inside her.

Last week, after we had sex for the second time in one damn day, she made sure that I left her house, before the thought of staying over could even cross my mind.

It's like she's trying to fight her attraction for me, when I know like hell, that she fucking loves my company.

I've done everything in my power to make sure of that and I don't plan to stop. Especially now that I've learned of her piece of shit ex.

Now that Lynx has stopped taking calls, and has made me the top Alpha, I've barely have time to breathe. Business is busy and all of the changes are only making it harder to have a free moment.

I haven't seen Karma since I spotted her at *Club Royal* a few days ago, dancing so damn sexy on that dance floor. She only gave me a few minutes of her time, before she left me standing with a damn hard-on, wanting more of her. She knew damn well what she was doing when she danced against me like she did. I could feel the sexual tension between us and I know she did too.

As much charm as I attempted to work on her, she refused to come back to the mansion with me, even to celebrate my damn promotion. When I told her that Lynx was moving me up to top Alpha so he could focus on his relationship with Rebel, she just smiled and simply said congratulations.

She mentioned how messed up her life is right now and that she needed space, so I did just that. I've given her a little time to think straight, but have still made it clear that she's to call me if that asshole ever enters her shop again.

I won't hesitate to rough his ass up and give him the ass kicking that he deserves.

"Hey you, blonde dick." Rome knocks on the door to my office and pokes his head inside. "We still having that group meeting in five? The guys are waiting and getting impatient as fuck. Some have calls lined up soon."

I turn around in my chair and place my hands behind my head with a smirk, enjoying my new position. "How does it feel, fucker? Never thought you'd be taking orders from my ass, did you? That's what happens when you know how to work your shit right," I tease, just to get under his skin.

"Fuck you, dumbass. Doesn't bother me any. My caller numbers have been rising like crazy this week. I've been taking so many calls that my dick hurts and shit. This is crazy and I love the fuck out of it."

I smile with a proud feeling of accomplishment for the House. "Damn straight. I've been promoting the hell out of the website and Lynx has had Rebel focusing on the same whenever she gets a chance."

"I'm not complaining." Rome laughs. "I saw that your ass even set up a Facebook page for the Alpha House. Have fun with that because the messages and comments will never stop on that page. Over two-hundred women have already posted on the damn wall."

I run my fingers through my beard and stand up, Alpha stretches and stands to follow me. "Over two hundred thousand likes in less than a week. Give it a month and see how much your dick hurts then. You think two-hundred posts on the wall is a lot, just wait until you see all of the messages that have already poured in since the other day. Most of them have already signed up and shared with their friends."

Rome looks behind him, when a wadded up pair of socks hits him on the shoulder.

"Get your asses down here," Knox yells from below. "I have a call in five minutes and I'm not missing this shit so we can stand around with our dicks in our hands for the fuck of it."

We both make our way downstairs, with Alpha at our feet, never missing the opportunity to be our entertainment at a group meeting.

"Alright, fuckers." I smirk, while crossing my arms over my chest. "I made a Facebook page for the Alpha House and I'm going to need you guys to help answer questions and run the page. It's a team effort and I need everyone on board to help keep this shit running smoothly. Lynx has already had me add everyone on as admins. There are a shit ton of messages and questions already so jump on that shit."

"That page is already blowing up and going crazy," Nash speaks up. "I've already added over a hundred callers to my wait list." He pulls the front of his cowboy hat down in the front and crosses his arms as he leans against the couch. "I like it and I'm always ready for a challenge. These women want a Southern gentleman that will give them what they want and that's what I'm here for."

"Alright," Levi agrees. "I'll check it in the mornings when I get up. Shit. As if I don't have enough to do. Don't expect us to be able to keep up though with our dicks in our hands most of the day."

Everyone else agrees, with a little bitching, to check in between their calls, ending the group meeting so everyone can get back to their calls.

"Alright, keep your schedules tight and let me know of any issues you have. Lynx won't be around to handle the day to day shit, so you're stuck with me. It should be pretty easy though, just don't do anything I wouldn't do."

The room fills up with laughter and I can see they all know that means shit is getting ready to get crazy in this house. These guys all know how to conduct business and keep things moving, money is one great motivator for that.

"Shit, if we all act like you, this place is going to be one hell of a fuck pad." They all begin to move out and I sit there with Alpha at my feet.

I have to admit that I sort of felt like King Shit for a few short minutes and I loved the hell out of it. Unfortunately, I still have my own calls to handle, so I take off before I have too much time to bask in the actual fact that this job is becoming a career to me.

I make it to my room with only a few minutes to spare before my next call.

Feeling happy and confident after our little group meeting, I change into my 'black tie affair' attire, letting my tie hang loosely around my neck. The women seemed to love this at the party.

I slip a pair of jeans on over my man-thong and grin as I turn on the camera.

Bigredandsassy immediately starts typing as I stand back and grip my tie, wrapping it around my fists.

Bigredandsassy: Oh my . . . what a way to get the night started.

You're new for me and I'm liking what I see so far. Turn around and let me see the rest of you.

Lifting a brow and smirking, I turn around to give her a view of my ass.

Bigredandsassy: I'm convinced that you're trying to kill me here with that fine ass of yours, Blaze. I want to bite it. Momma likes.

"Is that right?" I flash her a playful smile and grip the top of the black fabric, pulling it down a bit in the front. "Just wait until you see what else I've got."

Bigredandsassy: You're such a tease. I think you might just be my favorite now. So . . . why don't you lower those sexy thongs down more and show me what I'm missing out on.

Closing my eyes, I let my mind wander to Karma and the way she turned me on with each moan that left her beautiful lips. The way she dug her nails into my back as I buried myself deep had me about ready to blow inside her.

I feel myself getting hard, so I grab it through the fabric and stroke it a few times to make sure that it's ready for viewing.

My eyes open when the computer dings.

Bigredandsassy: Oh yes . . . I'm touching myself now, Blaze. I'm so damn turned on by watching you touch yourself. Keep going. Let me see you play with that big dick of yours as if you wish it were me.

Pulling my bottom lip between my teeth, I release my tie and grip my dick with both hands, slightly moaning as I picture Karma again.

Within seconds, I get so excited that I pull my dick out completely and begin stroking it as if no one is watching me.

I'm so distracted that I jump when the computer dings again.

> *Bigredandsassy: Yes! Keep going. Stroke that humongous dick. Fuck, this is so hot. Keep going. I'm about to come.*

Walking closer to the camera, I make sure that it's only my cock in view as I continue to stroke myself, knowing that I'm not going to be able to come, until I hurry up and get her off the line.

After a few more seconds, the computer dings again, so I step back so I can see what she typed.

> *Bigredandsassy: Oh my fuck! I've never come to hard in my life. Thank you! Really . . . thank YOU. I'll be a returning caller for sure. You've proven yourself to me and it was worth every single penny.*

I wink in the camera and smile, before quickly closing it and stroking my cock for my own pleasure this time.

Imagining the curves of Karma's perfect body and how every inch of her skin tasted against my tongue, my speed picks up, stroking my length until I feel a tug on my balls.

"Oh fuck!" I yell out as my come squirts all over my hand, coating it.

Fighting to catch my breath, I grab for a shirt and clean off, before jumping in the shower to chill the fuck out a minute. .

I really need to see this damn woman again. Holy fuck!

Chapter
EIGHT

Karma

I FIND MYSELF SMILING WHEN a text message from Blaze comes through, distracting me from the skeleton design I'm drawing up for a client. It's going to be two skeletons kissing on his upper back with their hands embracing each other's faces.

I drop my pencil on the desk as I reach for the phone.

"Just when I was starting to think your ass gave up." I laugh to myself and open his message.

> *Blaze: My call for tonight got canceled due to insufficient funds. You near a computer?*

> *Karma: Actually, I do have one nearby . . . but I happen to be busy.*

My smile broadens as I set my phone down and go back to concentrating on my sketch.

I should've known that he'd attempt to draw me in by one of his damn calls. He knows his body is hard to resist and he's right. Even though I don't want to give in to him, I have to admit that I'm curious to see what it's like to be on the other end of his call. Doesn't mean I plan to stop everything I'm doing to do so.

My phone goes off two more times, finally making me give in and look to see what else he has to say.

> Blaze: *I'm sure whatever you're doing can wait until after I make you come again.*

> Blaze: *Five minutes. Remember what I can do in five minutes. I made you an account. I'll text you the info.*

Well I can say one thing, this guy is persistent when he wants something and apparently he really wants this damn call to happen.

Tossing my pencil down *again*, I push my drawing aside and pull out my laptop and wait for it to start up.

My phone goes off a few seconds later with a username and password.

I hope he doesn't expect me to pay for this crap, because there's no way I'm paying seven hundred dollars for something I can easily see in real life.

Getting comfortable, I sit back in my chair and cross my legs on the desk in front of me. I'm just waiting for him to pop up and see what kind of surprises he has for me tonight since he always seems to.

I straighten in my seat and reach for my beer to cool off. Blaze appears on the screen, shirtless and wearing a pair of sweats. *When did sweats become sexy?* His hair is a hot mess and I'm tempted with the reminder of my hands in it as I rode his beard that first night. *Fuck that beard of his felt so good.*

The tired, messy look looks completely sexy on him.

"Well you got me here . . ." I smile as he rubs his chest and yawns. How in the world does he look so hot right now? "You going to entertain me or what? Better make this little call worth my time since I stopped working for this."

He stands up, smirks and pulls the front of his sweats down, revealing the muscles that lead down to the very big cock that I know he has. "Depends."

I laugh and watch him closely as he gets comfortable in his chair again. "On what, big guy?"

"If you're going to give me a little entertainment first." He playfully smiles into the camera and I catch myself smiling back.

My body instantly heats up at the idea of playing with myself on camera for him. Only for this guy would it turn me on so damn much.

Doesn't mean I won't make him beg a little first.

Standing up, I fan my face off, as if I'm hot. "Oh fuck . . ." I moan. "It's so hot in here." I grab the rip in the front of my thin shirt and rip it a little more down my breasts, holding it open so far that it's almost showing my nipples. Then I sit back and get comfortable just to tease him.

"Oh fuck," he growls and runs his hand down his abs, before grabbing his dick through his sweats. "Don't stop now. I'm completely hard."

"Do you feel how hot it is?" I tease. "It's. So. Fucking. Hot."

He grabs the computer and tilts it down more so that I can see him grabbing the bulge of his dick. "Not yet, baby. Show me."

Purposely pulling my bottom lip between my teeth, I hold a beer up and pour it down my breasts and the front of my body, soaking the white t-shirt.

My shirt clings to my breasts and my hard nipples are so close to being on display for him.

"Take it off, Karma," he says in a husky voice. "Take it off or I'm coming to do it myself."

I raise my brows in amusement and then slowly grab the rip

in my shirt and yank it open completely, before rubbing the beer over my nipples.

"Oh shit. I want to take those nipples in my mouth and nibble the fuck out of them."

"Now take your pants off, Blaze." I smirk and run my hand down the front of my body, until my fingers disappear into my panties. I tilt the computer down a bit to make sure he can see. "Isn't this how it works? Take those fucking pants off and stroke your big cock for me. Make this worth it for me."

Without hesitation, Blaze stands and pulls his sweats down all the way, making me suck in a breath of surprise when I see that he's not wearing anything underneath. I was expecting some kind of strip-tease first.

Holy shit . . . I want that in my mouth.

"You were right," I say out of breath.

He grabs his thick shaft and begins stroking it so damn good. "About what?"

"You're completely fucking hard."

"Touch yourself, Karma. Pretend that it's my pierced cock in that tight little pussy." He shakes his head as I slide a finger inside me. "You're going to have to use as least four fingers to pretend that it's me, baby."

I lean back in the chair and slowly pull out, before sliding two fingers inside. Even that is hard for me to do.

"I guess that will have to do since I'm not there." I look down at myself and get completely turned on when I see just how wet he has made me. "Look at me," he demands.

Slowly fingering myself, I look up at him to see him stroking his cock with both hands.

"Fuck me, Karma," he breathes out. "Ride those fingers as hard as you rode my dick."

His words have me completely losing my shit. "Ahhh . . ." I

moan and pick up my speed, just as he does.

"You like watching me stroke myself for you, Karma?"

I nod my head and lick my lower lip in concentration as I watch him.

"Tell me." He smirks and slows down his jerks, to give me a better view of his fingers running over the head of his dick.

Instead of telling him, I pull my fingers out of my pussy and give him a view of how wet I am for him.

"Oh shit, Karma." His strokes become faster as I lift my ass up off the chair to give him a better view and slowly slip my fingers back inside. "Keep going," he says deeply.

Feeling myself beginning to clench, I twirl my thumb over my clit and moan out as my orgasm rocks through me.

"Fuck! Fuck me!"

I look at the computer, out of breath, as I watch Blaze moan and cuss through his own orgasm. Seeing his come coat his tattooed hand and knowing that it's because of me is so fucking hot.

Feeling completely satisfied, I wipe my hands off on my wet shirt and watch as Blaze places a towel in his lap and watches me.

"Best call I've ever had," he brags.

I laugh. "I bet it was, playboy."

He jerks when the towel moves a little. "Holy fuck!"

"Calls over." I smile and lean in close. "You should get that cleaned up for your next caller. Bye."

"Karm-"

I hit the disconnect button before he can say anything, knowing damn well that he'll be finding my ass soon for sure now.

There's no way he's going to take me jerking and running well. It's just about as bad as the fucking and running that I did last week and forced him to leave the only other time.

I rush into the bathroom and turn on the shower water,

smiling the whole time as I replay our little video call.

That man is definitely going to make it more difficult than I expected. I have a feeling that Blaze is a man that gets what he wants.

I need to be careful with this one . . .

Chapter NINE

Blaze

MY HEAD'S COMPLETELY FUCKED TODAY and has been since I watched Karma finger fucking herself and then disappearing last night.

My twin brother Luca arrives today, so I've been trying to keep focused on getting his room set up and take care of things around the house. He'll be the newest guy in the house and I have no doubt he'll fit right in. He's my twin so it's in his damn blood to do well with this.

Lynx has been by a few times today to make sure that we don't need anything for the house and that everyone's staying busy, so my head's been all over the place.

"... Dude, you been listening to anything I've said?"

I shake my head to clear it and look up to see Rome setting up his computer down by the pool. "Fuck no. Sorry, man."

"I'm about to take a call, so unless you want to see my big dick, then you might want to leave the pool area."

Before I can even reply, he's shaking his cock in his hand, working on getting it ready for his chat.

"You can't give me a few seconds to leave first? Shit. I don't want to see that unless I'm getting paid to, fucker."

He laughs and hops into the water, being careful not to splash his computer. "That might be happening soon because I have a client that wants to see you, me and Levi. I tried to talk her out of it, but she's offering to pay a shit ton extra to see the three of us at the same time. Guess it's some fucked up fantasy of hers to have three men at once. I'm talking this is enough fucking money to work that one call that night and make more than most nights. Can't turn that kind of money down."

I nod my head and agree. As long as the guys keep their dick in their own vicinity, then I could care less about jerking around them. I'm not ashamed of my dick, in fact I'm proud of that fucker.

I've done a camera jerk with Lynx and Knox before that I definitely didn't think would be the last request for more than one guy.

"Fuck no we can't. Just give me the details once you get them worked out so I can make sure we don't have other calls overlapping."

Walking away, I pull out my phone and send Karma a text.

I wasn't done with her last night and I want her to know that.

Blaze: Enjoy my company too much last night?

Karma: Is that what you get from me logging off in a rush?

Her response makes me smile, because yes, it does. There's got to be some reason why she refuses to spend more time with me.

Blaze: I think I'm getting to you. I'm digging myself under your skin and you're afraid that you'll want me there.

Karma: The only place I want you, Blaze is in between my legs. I wouldn't worry too much about getting to me. It's not easy.

Blaze: I'll remember that.

I shove my phone in my pocket when my twin brother's handsome ass walks through the front door.

"Damn, I look good today," I tease Luca like I have my entire life.

"We're two different people, fucker. You don't get to claim my good looks." He smiles as he meets me with our usual hug, hitting me on the back once before he steps back. "But hell yeah, we look good all day, every day."

"Your fucking hair is long. Damn you have me wishing I had the patience to grow mine out." His hair is hanging down the side of his face and the sides are cut short. He can look clean or rough as fuck and damn I'm jealous of that.

"You know I have to have at least one thing that sets us apart." He looks past me at Rome who is still prepping for his call. His smile grows even larger as he realizes the ease of the fact that Rome is literally jerking off right here in front of us while we have a normal conversation.

"I can see this house is going to be interesting."

"Just wait until we have your welcome party. You don't even know what crazy is until you've been to one of our parties." He follows me into the kitchen where I hand him a shot glass and pour the tequila tall to initiate him properly.

"First we toast to you joining the house, then I'll show you around." We both lift our glasses over the bar, coming close to clinking before he pulls back.

"What the fuck? I imagined my first shot would be between a set of nice tits or off of some flawless skin . . ." The door opens before he finishes. I look over and see Lynx step inside with

Karma following closely behind.

"Now that's more fucking like it." Luca moves towards Karma and I stand to watch how it all unfolds, all the while fighting the urge to step between them and stop him from going near her.

Lynx reaches for Luca's hand, introducing himself and I don't hear what else is said because I'm looking at her. Her lips look full today, like she's showing off her perfect dick sucking lips for the world to see.

"Now, who is this?" He moves around Lynx, quickly stepping next to Karma.

"Luca, this is Karma. She's a tattoo artist and the one that pierced all of us recently. We work with her shop for promotions." His stupid ass grin irritates me, but she calms me just slightly by taking a step back from his forward advancing ass.

"Yes. You'll have to have your brother bring you by my shop and I'll treat you to the same if you're interested." She looks over at me with a small smile and I stand proud knowing she's not falling for his smooth game. I've seen many fall for it, hell he's just like me when it comes to getting the women.

"You see, I've had my dick pierced for years, but if you're going to do it, I'll get another one." He runs his hands through his hair and I catch him give her the look. The damn look that I use to reel in a girl I want to fuck.

She stops moving and watches him closely. I can tell she's interested and that shit pisses me off more than I'd like to fucking admit. I have no right to be upset, but I am.

Lynx pulls up a bar stool and reaches for the bottle of tequila.

"Are you really going to stand there with your dick in your hands and not share that bottle." He leans back and takes a swig, getting Karma's attention when he does.

"Are we meeting in your office this time?" She starts to walk out of the kitchen, leaving the two of us watching her ass as she walks.

"Let's meet outside by the pool." Lynx stands and before I have the chance to stop them from going out there with Rome, Luca stops them.

"Rome is taking a call out there right now. You might want to pick somewhere else."

Karma stops quickly and turns, looking flushed. "Jesus, this house is insane. How do you even live here?"

Her question is aimed at Lynx, who quickly replies as he walks out of the room with her.

"I don't anymore, but it's not that bad. It's business mostly and the money more than makes up for any issues any of us have."

I stare at Luca and watch him take in my facial expression before he starts laughing.

We share a silent exchange before Lynx yells from the stairs. "Blaze. Luca . . . why don't you join us for this meeting."

"Let me guess, you've called shotgun on her." Luca gives me a look like he already knows the shotgun rule is in play. This is something we've always done. If one of us has any depth of feeling toward a girl, we say shotgun and the other one stays away. I actually think he started it when we were like twelve and both had our eyes on some little blonde in our class.

He can pick up what I'm feeling about Karma even though I don't want it out there. *Fuck.* This is that bad part about having a twin, you never really get any privacy.

"You can say that." His laughter echoes around me as we hit the main foyer and is still going when I lead us up the stairs.

"My brother has been whipped by the pussy fairy. I've been waiting on this day."

"Shhhh. What the fuck is wrong with you? I'm not

whipped." I turn to quiet him before his damn deep voice carries through the house. A roaring deep voice is about the only characteristic that we both got from our asshole father.

We step through the office door and I stand off to the side of Lynx's desk and Luca takes the other.

"Alright. What I've been thinking, Karma I'd like to offer you a room to do work in a few nights a week and stream out the live feed to clients who want to view. Of course, this would have to be approved by the person getting the work done. Hell, we could even offer them their work for free if it all pays out like I'm expecting."

"What kind of split are you thinking?" She instantly responds and I can see she's curious about what he has to say.

"We can split evenly, but if any of my guys are in the room we'll need to split an equal share with them because it'll be because they're getting work done that the viewer count would be through the roof." She looks at me just as he finishes and doesn't give a hint of what she's thinking in the look on her face.

"I'm not sure this is a good move for my shop, Lynx. You'll have to give me a few days to think on it." She sits confidently across from him while she talks business and I'm a dick for thinking she's sexy as fuck for the way she's conducting business with Lynx.

I watch Lynx lean back in his chair and cross his arms while he takes in her response.

"What's to think about? It's exposure and other than the releases from clients that you'd need to obtain, it should be a no brainer."

She matches his demeanor and sits back against the back of her chair, crossing her sexy legs in that skirt that now has my attention.

Her leg tattoo is partially hidden and yet again I feel myself frustrated that I haven't had the time to properly see all of the art her body carries.

She's fucking gorgeous and it's been a long ass time since a woman has gotten to me like she has. Maybe even the first time.

Fuck, I need to get my hands on her again soon. Soon as in before she leaves this fucking house.

Chapter TEN

Karma

I CAN FEEL BLAZE WATCHING me closely, so I purposely tease him. Lynx is all business and I can't even deal with the way Blaze's twin was staring me down in the kitchen.

It's not fair to have two of them in the world and if I hadn't always wanted to mess with a set of twins, I fucking do now.

I need to stop thinking like this. I'm fighting the urge to squirm in my chair with this much sexiness around me.

"I can appreciate that. Think on it and get back with me. I know we can work well together to hit a new audience for us and in the process have them rolling in to your shop for work." Lynx sounds confident that this is the right move, but I don't know yet. I might need more information to convince me. I start to think about the increase in business so far with the small amount of promoting we've done and know my problem will be not having enough artists to handle the load.

"I'll need to confirm a few new artists before I can even consider taking on something like this."

Lynx leans forward on his desk and begins to work on his computer.

"I have a few guys in mind that would do well for your shop. I'll see if they're interested in moving and send them your way."

I watch Blaze move around behind Lynx before he begins talking. "You know we could do the live feed to more than one caller, that would maximize profits for her call and easily make Karma and the house a shit ton of money. We wouldn't have any sexual acts through that feed, but they'd get to see live piercings of anything we set up and of course we could run a special tattoo night. It could be like one night a week until we see if it works well."

He surprises me with his insight and I like what he's suggesting. My interest is definitely piqued now. "Hell, we could just do a trial run this week to see if any of the viewers are interested in tapping in to something like that before we lock into anything on either side of this agreement." Blaze's business side comes out and he honestly surprises me with it. Hell, even his posture has changed. It's like he's morphed into some CEO or something as he takes over the room with his personality.

I really do love what he's saying. It gives me a chance to see how I like it before I commit to new artists and such a change for my shop.

"Is this your way of getting me inside this house again?" I have to tease him and make him stop acting like a boss. Honestly, it's getting to me in more ways than one. He smiles as I give him hell. "Let me guess, you'll offer up your room for me to do my trial night."

"Hell, I'll offer my body for you to work on that first night. Can you imagine the callers that would want to see you work on me?" Blaze looks so proud of his suggestion before Luca begins to speak.

"How about we add the twin aspect to this lil' show? If you want viewers, bust that shit out and watch it rain fucking dollar signs all around us." Luca surprises the entire room when he begins to speak.

I catch Blaze's death glare in his direction, but notice Luca isn't even looking Blaze's way. *He's looking at my tits.*

"I like the thought of it raining cash, hell we need to make this as successful as we can for as long as we can, because we all know this isn't something we can all do 'til we retire. No one wants to see a shriveled old dick on the screen." Lynx stands to pace behind the desk a few times.

"I'm not sure how your dick is looking, but I'm pretty sure I'm good for let's say . . . the rest of my fucking life. This cock will never shrivel. I'll make sure of that shit." Blaze finally comes around to the conversation again and I can see the fun side of him resurface even if it's something he's forcing himself to do.

This is exactly what I didn't want. I don't want him getting too attached to the idea of me. He's feeling territorial and that's when I'm known to step. I don't need someone to think they own me like a piece of fucking property. I had enough of that when I was with Ryan.

I take care of myself and when it comes to men, I won't be tied down to another one. *No matter how damn sexy he is.*

"Let's set it up for later this week then. I'll have Rebel put out an advertisement and get some callers on board." Lynx looks to Blaze. "Looks like you'll be the test dummy on this shit so you can push and get some of your viewers involved. Jump on the Alpha's Facebook page and promote the fuck out of it. I'll have Rebel send out a mass email to the subscriber list and we'll just see what happens."

I stand up and look around the room, taking in the masculinity around me. Most women wouldn't even be able to handle being in this room right now without jumping on one of them. Me . . . I'm a little stronger . . . even with Blaze looking at me like he is. "Boys . . ." I smirk at Blaze as his eyes follow me to the door. "We'll be in touch. I've got some other dicks to pierce for some strippers a town over. Lucky me."

Luca begins walking as if he's going to approach me, but Blaze is quick to snap his arm out and stop him. "Better slow your fucking roll, bro." He gives Luca a hard look and then follows me out the door as if he's going with me.

I stop and turn around when he keeps following me. "What are you doing?"

"Going with you to make sure these *dicks* don't get out of line. You came here alone to a damn house with ten horny ass guys and asked us all to whip our dicks out. The Alpha House is under a lot more control than these wild ass strippers you're about to go see."

As much as I don't want him thinking that I need him to protect me, he's right about this one. I've met a few of these male entertainers before; every single one of them thought I was going to fuck one of them before the night was over.

"Fine. You can come but just stay back. I can handle my damn self, Blaze."

"I'm out!" he yells down the hall. "I'll help set Luca's work station up when I get back. Let's go." He doesn't even wait for a reply, before he grabs my hand and pulls me down the stairs with him.

I smile and shake my head as he runs over to the car and holds the door open for me. "So damn smooth, aren't you, Blaze?"

He shrugs and proudly lifts a brow, while watching me get in the vehicle. "Fuck yes I am. I'll follow you."

I start the car and wait for Blaze to pull his truck around and follow me to the strip club.

This should be interesting . . .

Chapter
ELEVEN

Karma

HE PULLS UP BEHIND ME and immediately jumps out to help me with my equipment case.

"Well this shit should be interesting. It's not as if I don't see enough *dick* as it is. The things I do for a fine as hell woman."

I look him over as he opens the back door to let us in. "Would you mind holding, while I pierce?" I tease, just to see how far I can push him 'til he pushes back. It's a little game we play and I've honestly missed it when we aren't after each other like this.

"Well damn. Keep looking at me like that, and I'll hold anything you want as long as I get to take you to my bed after and remind you what a real cock looks like."

A blonde guy who has to be in his late forties greets us and takes us back to a room where his guys are waiting. There are only six of them so I hope this goes quickly.

They're all standing around, half-naked, most of them looking as if they just woke up for the day. Guess they had a late ass night.

"The name is Hale," the older guy speaks. "I'll be in my

office if you need me for anything. The guys will tell you what they want. Evan is my main guy so I'll let him take over." He points to Even. "I got some work to take care of."

"Sounds good," I say before he walks away.

Having Blaze's eyes on me isn't going to make this the slightest bit comfortable, knowing that he's probably thinking about ripping every one of these stripper's dicks off because I'm touching them.

He tries to play it off, but by the way he keeps cracking his neck, and intimating the other guys, I know he's disliking this set up.

After my equipment is set up, Blaze pulls out a stool and sits back, but stays close enough to let the guys know that he's here.

I point to their main entertainer Evan. "You first. Drop your pants and tell me what you want."

He gives me a look, showing me what he's thinking, but Blaze's evil glare wipes the smug look right off his face. I can see why Blaze is watching him extra careful, because this guy is the definition of pretty: long blonde hair, tall and lean with just the right amount of muscle. He's definitely the best looking guy in the room other than Blaze.

"Whatever you think works. You're in charge," he finally says. "Give me something the women will love."

"Give him something small. You want to still be able to see his dick behind the metal." Blaze lifts a brow in concern and pulls out a protein bar when Evan drops his pants. He takes a bite and laughs around it, as if we can't hear him.

His dick is average size, but of course Blaze just has to open his big mouth and show his displeasure.

"Fuck off. It's cold in here. There's nothing small about my dick." He sits up and looks at me as I let out a small laugh. "Trust me. I've never had a complaint, babe."

I place my hand on his shoulder and push him back down, trying to keep my composure. "Ignore him. His dick is larger than the average human so everything looks small to him."

I catch Blaze smirk from me having just admitted it out loud. Hopefully he'll calm the hell down now that I've announced that he's superior to most.

Ass.

He seems to quiet down after that. He's actually letting me do my job without pissing these guys off any more than he already has.

Yeah, most of them are smaller than the men at the Alpha House, but still average and nothing to be ashamed of.

All except for the last guy. I even have to keep myself from laughing and asking how the hell he's even in this line of business.

He has a good looking face and a decent body, but seriously. I feel bad for the guy. *Maybe he stuffs his underwear.*

I wait for Blaze to say something, but he keeps his mouth closed, until *right* after I get done and the poor guy stands up to pull his pants back up.

"I have no words," Blaze mumbles. "No fucking words."

I shoot him a glare and mouth for him to shut up before he makes me lose business.

Luckily, Hale walks into the room and calls his guys away before anything can be exchanged between the guys and Blaze.

Music is coming from the next room now, so my guess is that these guys will be dancing any minute now and maybe even showing off their new piercings. I know they show more than they're supposed to at these clubs. It's no secret.

I glare at Blaze with my most pissed off look and he just smiles. I pop one of the gloves against my wrist before I remove them both, never looking away from him. He has to know he crossed lines with these guys.

As soon as we get outside to my car, I place my hand over Blaze's mouth and get in his face. "What the hell! You could've just lost me business in there. You can't say that kind of shit to my clients, just like you have to accept all of yours equally. They pay my fucking bills, Blaze. Not cool."

He takes this opportunity to bite my hand and pick me up as if this is some kind of fun game. "I call out what I see." He smiles against my lips. "They call those guys entertainment. I could've said a whole lot more. Trust me. I have jokes for days."

I slide down his thick body and walk him backwards, until he's pressed against his truck. Then I grab his dick and squeeze it. "Good thing you didn't." I press my lips against his neck, before running them up to stop below his ear. "It might've been a long time before I'd touch this beautiful thing again. Remember that for next time." I remove my hand with haste to prove a point.

"You sure about that?" he asks with confidence.

"Positive. I have a lot of restraint when it's necessary."

Smiling in satisfaction from the look on Blaze's face, I walk away and jump into my car, taking off before Blaze can try to follow me.

I don't know if I can handle any more of his sexy ass today . . .

Chapter
TWELVE

Blaze

I'VE OFFICIALLY LOST MY MIND. Tonight is the live feed with Karma and I guess my twin brother will be making his first appearance.

The sales for it have surpassed what we thought possible and I'm not sure if it's because people want to see me lose my shit about another piercing, or if they're excited about meeting Luca.

I have to admit they seem to love me in this industry and I can imagine that they're all foaming at the mouth to get a glimpse of him too. It's been interesting growing up with a twin and I'm sure this house will prove to be the same.

We've had our times of loving the twin thing and then despised it at others. He was so much like me that I honestly wanted to kick his ass for it. I guess we can thank our older brother for throwing us into the party scene at an early age.

He was always the life of the party and someone we both looked up to. Then when he went into the military we continued his legacy by both being the life of the party.

I can't tell you how many women we've been through or how many of them wanted us at the same time. It's most women's fantasy so you can say I've been admired and targeted since a young age.

Karma's little comment isn't going to fly with me though. We've never fucked a woman at the same time and I don't plan to start, especially with her. No fucking way am I sharing her. Hell, I can't even get her to last as long as I need her to so I can get over the urge to fuck her, just like I easily did with all the others before her.

The way I look at it, it's my job to thoroughly exhaust her, so what would be the purpose of having my brother there? To actually sword fight my way into one of her tight holes, because there's no doubt that's what we'd both be focused on.

Besides that, he's my fucking brother. I don't need that shit in my bed. My dick has always been more than enough for the women I've been with. Hell, I don't even fit all the way in most.

I've heard the screams of pleasure from his women over the years, I can only imagine that he's just as blessed in that department and will want to run the show just like I do.

It would only be a battle for power and that shit doesn't even sound appealing against him.

I decide to call Karma to prepare myself for what she has lined up for tonight's show. It seems like it'll be a short one, but who knows what all will go down once you get the three of us behind the camera. I can only imagine the comedy side of this will be obvious to all of those watching.

"Hey," I say when she picks up. "What time will you be here to set up? I've cleared my room for you to use tonight and also had my callers moved back so I can help keep it entertaining."

She laughs into the phone and the sound goes straight through me. Fuck, it's so sexy.

"I'm headed there now. I have to set up the table and all of my equipment beforehand. I thought I could do that before I get ready, if that's alright. Then I'll come back when it's time to go live."

I'm excited to hear that she's coming early. To be honest, she's been on my mind since yesterday when I was with her for the strippers' piercings. She's actually been on my mind since the Black Tie party, but who's counting.

"Sounds great. I'll see you when you get here." I end the call and smirk.

She had to have heard the enthusiasm in my voice, but I don't care. I've never tried to hide what she does to me. There's no point in trying.

"You ready for this? After tonight you'll officially have some fucking competition in this house." Luca walks into the kitchen with his towel around his waist, barely holding up. His wet hair is slicked back from an obvious swim and he tracks in water as he walks around me.

"Did you even dry off before you dripped your way into the house?" He begins to laugh when Alpha starts to lick up his puddles.

"I just need a water and I'm headed back out there. You should really work on that tan of yours before tonight's show. I'm gonna show you up if you don't."

I look down at my stomach and compare it to his. He's just a little darker than I am.

"You're funny as hell. Do you not realize that I'm doing just fine in this industry without your competition to push me?"

He turns and looks at me before he makes it to the door.

"I didn't say you needed a boost. Just thought you'd want to take in some sun with your fucking twin, but never mind." He walks out the door, shutting it hard behind him and I instantly feel bad for being shitty lately.

I haven't exactly been real welcoming to Luca so far. He

sealed the deal on that with his damn reaction to Karma, knowing that I'm interested in her. I know she's a soft spot for me, but I don't intend to ruin a relationship with my brother over it.

I grab two beers and pop the tops off of them before I slide the door open and step out. He's already in the pool again lying on a blue floating mattress, looking as if he doesn't have a care in the fucking world. He's always been good at being the happy one that doesn't let shit get to him.

Stepping next to the water, I lean over and hand him one of the bottles.

"Get ready asshole, me and my big dick will be getting in the pool."

His laughter echoes across the water and I can see the reflection of myself in his glasses as he sits up.

"Thanks for the warning. Wouldn't want to get a surprise like that and be thrown clear out of the fucking pool. You know, since we're twins and all I have no idea what you're packin'."

I slide my glasses off the collar of my t-shirt and put them on my face.

Tossing my shirt and shorts to the side, I walk to the stairs of the pool in my lime green tiny swim shorts. If there's one thing I've learned in this house, be prepared to swim at all times.

I spread out on the other large mattress and let the sun begin to do its thing. The music in the background makes for a relaxing moment and I embrace the silence, until he begins to talk.

"So. About this girl. How off limits is she?"

"Very." I close my eyes and wait for his next poke at me.

"I can tell and to be honest, it was fun riling you up the other day. Just know I'd never even cross that line, but that doesn't mean I won't torture you a little before."

He downs his beer and leaves the pool to get more, no doubt tracking in more water as he does. This time he brings two beers a piece, tossing mine at me before he gets in.

I down my first one and open the next while he gets situated again.

"How are you gonna handle her piercing me tonight?" He's watching my reaction and I can honestly say it won't bother me if I know he's not going to attempt to make it any more than it needs to be during the show.

"I'll be fine. She does it for a living." The words come out of my mouth, but I'm not even sure if I believe them my damn self.

"It'll be interesting doing all of this with a large audience for my first time. I've watched a few of your promotional teases to try and figure out how all of this will work for me, not that any of those reassured me any. I just hope I'm cut out for this."

"Get through the first night, then get that fucking pay check . . . Then all of your doubts will disappear. I fucking promise." I continue to try to make him understand the benefits of this industry. "The one and only reason that I do this is the easy money that rolls in unlike any other job I've ever heard of, even stripping. This is a safer atmosphere and one where I get to pretty much be my own boss and set my own hours. This will be a fucking dream job for you, brother."

"I'm sure the pussy is just a bonus." His deep laughter is interrupted by the door sliding open and Karma strolling out looking sexier than ever.

"Let's just say that some of it is a bonus and some of it you just can't ever unsee. You have to make them all feel special on the other side of that camera, but only take the ones that do it for ya to your bedroom."

I take in Karma's full body as she stands at the edge of the pool, looking down at us. "You look hot as fuck." I can't resist saying what I'm thinking when it comes to her. My dick is twitching thinking about sliding her straps off her shoulders and letting that tiny little dress fall to the ground around her tall heels.

"This would be one hell of a promotional picture for this house. The two of you laid out like this. Damn sexy, boys," she says with a grin.

"The view I'm looking at is much better. Damn fuckin' sexy, woman. Why don't you climb on and we can give this mattress a test ride." She smirks as I pat my hand beside me.

"In your dreams, Blaze."

"Do you have any idea how fucked up my dreams are with you? I hope to fuck you actually do meet me there one day."

The sun shines around her and I can see the outline of her body through the material. Her legs stand parted and the temptation to move to her and slide my hands up those sexy legs is almost too much.

I let my eyes brush over her tattoos and further my pull toward her standing there. "Why don't you meet me upstairs and let me see all those tattoos you're hiding under that dress."

"It isn't my fault you didn't pay closer attention when you had the chance. Now help me get this station set up so we can do this show tonight." Her feistiness only makes things worse and I can feel my sexual frustration sky rocket as she walks away, swaying those sexy hips like she always does.

My brother's laughter gets louder and the smile on my face grows while I step out of the pool and prepare myself to be in a room with her.

We will fuck again and I will trace every one of those fucking tattoos. The only question is when.

Chapter

THIRTEEN

Karma

TONIGHT WILL BE INSANE AND I honestly can't wait to get this part of my marketing started. It's something new for me and the best part is I haven't had to invest a shit ton into this to test it out.

Blaze's room is all set up at the Alpha House and all I have to do is show up soon and get this started and somehow resist Blaze's constant attempts to get to me. If he only knew how much he affects me, he'd never leave me alone.

Rebel told me the sales for the show have been phenomenal and I know we're about to share some great cash flow. I'm genuinely excited for this idea now. This will help me get my shop ready for the growth I've been wanting to have. Money has really been all I've needed to make great things happen with my shop.

"Alright, are you sure you don't want me there to help hold one of those dicks? You know a girl would take one for the team just this one time." Charlie has been joking about this whole thing since I told her the idea. She loves it, just thinks it's crazy that the guys from the Alpha House will be doing something like it. She had a point that they can't be truly doing this for the money. That should be the one thing they're not lacking. I guess Blaze is doing this to truly help me get my show the initial viewers I need to make it a weekly one.

He's definitely got a lot of qualities I find myself enjoying.

These guys are no doubt more attractive than most of the men we see come in the shop, but that doesn't matter to me. I'll work on any person, but the viewers will want people that look like these guys. I'm not an idiot. Sex sells, and these guys are both the definition of hot as hell sex.

In my line of work most of it is done behind depth and meaning. If it's not that, they are simply wanting to be a canvas to be displayed for the world to appreciate. I can relate to both. All of my tattoos mean something to me and reflect something of my past.

"I bet you would take one for the team." I tease her back and pick up the extra gun I needed as backup for tonight.

"I'll take the long haired one. I know you have a thing for Blaze anyway." She causes me to stop in my tracks and question her.

"What makes you think so?"

"A blind person would feel the shift in the air and know you two are near each other. It's like one of those instant heavy feelings of chemistry in the air."

My laughter interrupts her from going on any further. I'm not sure I want to hear what else she is *sure* of about Blaze and I. She might just read through me even further and see shit I'm not ready to acknowledge.

"Are you sure it isn't his confidence lingering over everyone as he takes over the room? A man like Blaze is capable of many things."

"I'm positive," she says with a grin. "You can deny it all you want, but you have it bad for that guy."

I don't deny it, but I also don't confirm it. It's better to just walk away from Charlie in a battle like this.

"See you tomorrow. I need to get back to the house before they go live without me. That definitely wouldn't be good for business."

"Get him pierced where it really counts then, if you're gonna be riding that. I know he's only laddered . . . he needs that G-spot tingler," she yells at me as I walk out the door, and I won't turn around and tell her that the guy doesn't need any help in that department at all.

He can hit the perfect spot without any added jewelry to the tip. He's proved that more times than once.

Fuck me. I need to stop thinking about the details of his dick and be professional for this show. I hope he doesn't say things to make me blush, but knowing him, he will. And that says a lot about his mouth, because I don't blush. He just has a way of making it happen over and over. I need to be prepared for when he does so I don't give him a real look at how I feel about what he says to me.

I think about all the possibilities that could come out of his mouth during this and it's almost so much that I want to turn around and go home. He's a complete smart ass and that's one of the reasons he's so popular, so he'll have to be in true character tonight. The Blaze behind the camera is even more bold than the one I've been dealing with and that terrifies me just a little.

Plus Luca will be trying to get noticed over the large personality that is Blaze, so who knows what he'll say or do to make himself more popular to the viewers. The two of them together will be a damn powerhouse.

"What in the hell have I gotten myself into?" I can't hold my thoughts in any longer as I park in what seems like a truck dealership. The Alpha men all love their toys and they have the money to splurge on things like that, so I don't blame them, but damn can they not get the largest meanest trucks out there?

I see Blaze walking toward me before I can even get out of my car. He can probably guess that I'm unsure as hell about all of this, which would explain his smile on his face as he gets closer.

"It's about time to let people watch you stroke my dick. Who would've thought we'd be making porn so early in our relationship?" *That mouth of his. Damn that mouth.*

"I'm not stroking your dick on camera. And there is no relationship. We have to keep this professional when it comes to my feeds. I don't need assholes thinking they can come to my shop for some fucked up sex crap. The bell on the door would never stop dinging."

"I agree, but what would this be if I didn't come on to you? It's what I do." He wraps his arms around me before I'm able to reach in for the last box of my stuff.

"You need to stop looking so fucking sexy. Those have to be the shortest jean shorts I've seen in my life and your tits in that tank top are just begging me to dive in. Tell me, Karma, how am I supposed to keep my hands off of you when you look like this?" He runs his hands over my ass when I bend over.

I close my eyes with the feel of his hands on me again. This man knows how to make me feel like I'm the sexiest woman alive. I'm sure it's a trait he's learned gets him paid very well.

"Blaze. You have to stop doing this." I stand quickly before he has the chance to touch me where there'd be no turning back.

"What's the fun in that?" He runs his hands over my back and pulls me closer with his hands full of my ass. I really have no choice but to wrap my arms around his waist and melt into him. Well, maybe I had a choice, but my body didn't think so.

"We have less than fifteen minutes before we go live. As much as I'd love to skip the whole show, we'd piss off a shit ton of people who are looking forward to you torturing me on camera."

He steps away and pulls the box out of my car before he leads us into the back door of the house. I watch his ass as he takes the stairs. I can tell he knows I'm watching by the way he laughs.

"Luca will be up in a minute, but I figured you could start with me. We'll open it up for any questions to start with and let you work on me. He can direct the questions during that, then when it's his turn, we'll switch."

"Sounds like a plan." We work side by side getting the last of my equipment in place and just before it's time to go live, Luca walks in with a huge ass grin.

"Hell yeah. Let's get this party started." He claps his hands and then rubs them together in excitement.

Smiling at Luca with confidence, Blaze turns on the camera and starts the show.

"Hello everyone. Welcome to our first ever live feed with Karma from the K'inked House. She has agreed to team up with the Alpha House and we plan to give you one night a week where we bring in her clients and let you pay to watch. As the show goes on tonight, be sure to blast any questions our way and we'll do our best to answer." Blaze isn't the least bit shy in front of the camera and it shows one hundred percent.

"Also, it is with great pleasure that I get to introduce you all to my twin brother Luca, who is officially joining the Alpha House. His client roster will fill up fast, so once the show is over tonight, if you're interested in seeing more of this beast, make an appointment to see what he has to offer."

I can see the comments and questions rolling in and an overwhelming feeling instantly consumes me as I read a few.

I'm not one to love a crowd, where it seems like Blaze

handles it perfectly. It's extremely sexy and I'm going to enjoy watching him handle himself.

Luca lets out a deep, sexy laugh as he leans into the computer and skims through the questions. "No, I won't be stroking my dick tonight on camera, but I promise to give you a fan-fuck-ing-tastic show if you book a call with me after this." His eyes widen as he looks to answer the next question. "And yes my cock is just as good as Blaze's." He winks. "Again, you can see for your-self when you book with me."

Blaze nods at Luca to continue and introduce himself.

"Hi everyone, I'm Luca as you've just figured out. Don't judge me based on this guy. He likes to pretend he's hot shit, but I know him personally." Blaze turns to interrupt Luca, causing him to laugh before he continues. "No really, he's a great guy and I'll be honest, the idea of being on camera scares the shit out of me where he thrives on it. So don't be harsh on me if I suck at all of this tonight."

I watch so many comments roll on about how there's no way he can be terrible with his looks. Some are calling him dad-dy, where as others are just simply welcoming him to the house.

Blaze smirks as comments begin rolling in about how good Blaze is and how they've been waiting for weeks to get another show with him. Ignoring the comments, he begins talking. "So tonight, Luca and I are both getting pierced, but in future shows, Karma will be doing some tattoos and pulling in some of the other Alpha guys as well as her own clients to show you some of the detail that goes into her work."

"I've decided I'll just add one more bar, since I already have three dick piercings. Luca, what are you here for?"

"I'm in for the Apa or whatever she decides would be the best with the one I already have." I haven't even spoken yet and I know I need to get their attention quick to make this all successful and keep them coming back for more. I feel the urge to push away any reservations and come out blaring with a personality that'll sell, so that's what I do.

"Alright viewers, maybe we need to see this before we can make a decision; pants off, boys," I demand and feel a rush of relief when I seem to say it all with confidence. Now it's time to work and do what I could do in my sleep. I'll just add a cocky mouth to it all and be feisty. If nothing else, I know it'll get to Blaze in a way that wouldn't bother me one bit.

And finally I'm in my element.

"You want us stripped down at the same time?" Blaze sounds surprised by my demand. Look at that. For the first time he's not smiling and trying to come on to me.

"I mean you're twins, why wouldn't we want to see you side by side? I'm sure this is what our viewers are waiting for."

The look on their faces pulls a grin from me.

They both begin to slide their underwear down and I try not to gasp at them both. *Staying focused is crucial, Karma. Stay fucking focused.*

"Hold them so we can see the piercings."

The comments begin rolling in faster than before as they both grab their dicks and hold them out for the camera to see.

They're both hung and I'm not trying to compare or anything, but damn it they are truly identical twins all the way down to the tips of their dicks.

"Luca, you have a single bar. Do you want me to give you two more and then you can match Blaze?"

Luca laughs and releases his dick. "I've spent my entire life looking like his ass, why would I do that with my dick? Give me something on the tip."

"Well, that's what I was going to do, so I guess you can pierce both of my nipples instead." Blaze begins to back out of a dick piercing and I can honestly say, I'm not sure I could handle it if he had another one. Not that this is about me, but shit a girl can only handle so much.

"We can do that. You could always change your mind some other time and we can bring you back on for it."

He looks relaxed instantly, and I wait for his playful behavior to hit the room. I know it's coming.

"Besides that, I plan to use mine tonight and I'm not prepared to let some metal get in the way of the sweet pussy I plan to be balls deep in."

There it is. *Oh. My. God.*

I glare at him with my back to the camera as I begin to prepare my table for Luca. He smiles like he won this little show, but he has no idea how hard I can play.

"Alright, Luca, let's get you a Prince Albert and watch the ladies fall all over you even more than I'm sure they already do."

I watch Blaze slide his pants up and he catches my smirk as I reach for Luca and hold him in my hand. The things that man makes me want to do.

I'm holding his twin's dick in my hands and it's Blaze that I'm checking out.

Keep this professional. Keep this professional.

I catch Luca look up at me and wink, right before I slide the needle through and he bites his bottom lip from the pain. "Fuck me, this is ridiculous!" he screams out in a reaction I wasn't quite ready for. He seemed so calm to start with, but not so much now. He's breathing loudly and it takes a lot for me not to laugh at his irrational verbiage. Wow, he really is just like Blaze. As if one of him isn't enough.

He finally quiets down so I can finish it up. "Fuck, I kind of liked that," Luca says, looking up at me as I hold him in my hand and clean him off. He's obviously not talking about the piercing, but I refuse to acknowledge what he really means.

I can feel Blaze's eyes on the both of us as if he's waiting for a reaction. Well, I don't plan to give him one.

Blaze and Luca take over, answering questions and bickering with each other as I clean up and prepare to pierce Blaze's nipples.

"You all saw my pussy ass brother screaming live on his first night. I promise I'll coach him on what is actually attractive to the people who pay good money to see us."

"Should we tell them how you acted when I first met you?" I have to remind Blaze how he reacted when I pierced him. He wasn't pleased with the set up and it surprised me that he actually went through with it.

"Well, I thought we weren't talking about you drooling over my dick that first day. You wanted to keep that a secret." His ass is smiling and I want to strangle him. I compose myself and prepare a response that is deserved.

"A dick is a dick. I've seen many in my line of business and I promise you, it doesn't take a specific one to hit the spot." Oh shit. His facial expression is challenging and I instantly regret playing games with him in front of a live audience.

"Is that right? Hmm, that's not what you sounded like when I was deep . . ."

"Alright. Who is ready to see my dick in action? Sign up for my call list quick and be the first to help me work this one out. Karma has worked her magic on me and I can't stand this much longer. Guess I'm a guy glutton for punishment." Luca takes the monitor and pulls it directly toward him. He talks closely to the mic and seems to be helping me save some sort of face in this.

Blaze looks at me with a proud face thinking he defeated me in this. I want to torture him for what he just did, but at the same time I want to let him follow through with the dirty thoughts I know he's thinking.

Luca ends the call and looks at us both. He busts out laughing and Blaze follows. I don't follow what's so funny, but Luca quickly adds to the tension in the room.

"You two should just fuck on camera. Your banter back and forth is intense and that's the shit that's going to be the number one request for this show. You should've seen some of the comments rolling in."

"He will *never* be live with me again. I specifically said I needed this to appear professional and that is not how it turned out. Now I'll have idiots banging on the door trying to get in to the porn house that does tattoos. Damn it." I stand and start slamming my things into my bag. I'm frustrated as shit at Blaze.

Both of the guys stand and walk toward me. I can't deal with two of them. "Stop. Don't. Just let me get the hell out of here and try to think of a way to fix this." They both stop mid step and watch me.

"You have to admit it was a great show. People will come back for the next one, so we accomplished what we set out to do," Blaze starts in, only to have Luca follow right behind.

"They will definitely be back for more. Don't get your panties in a wad until you've seen what you just made. I have a feeling you'll get over anything you're pissed about now."

"I need to stay professional. I told you that." I stare at Blaze and he looks down as I talk. I know he gets my point and I just need to end this conversation. He shouldn't be able to get to me looking down and he does. He gets to me in everything he does and for that reason alone I need to get the hell out of here and only come to this house for business. It's safest that way.

I know one thing after tonight. *These boys are in for a lot of money having them both in this damn business . . . Holy shit.*

Chapter
FOURTEEN

Blaze

SHE'S DRIVING ME FUCKING CRAZY. She just left the house after our show. I was hoping to spend more time with her, but she apparently wants to make me insane, so she left in a hurry. I know I pissed her off, but it was just all in fun.

I'm just about to follow her ass and remind her why she shouldn't leave me in such a rush, when my phone rings. It's Lynx, which means work is about to get in the way of me apologizing and the fun my dick wants to have after. *Make up sex is fucking great.*

"I need you at *Club Royal* ASAP. Some stupid asshole is trying to tear the place up and Envy called the police. I can't get there as soon as you'd be able to." He sounds frantic and to be honest, I've been itching to beat the shit out of an asshole since I dealt with Karma's ex.

"On my way." I hang up before I take off like a bat out of hell. I'm only a few miles from the club, so it doesn't take me long to pull up to the disaster getting worse before my eyes.

Women are scattered outside, looking scared for their damn lives. Pushing through them to get inside, I look for Envy or any of the girls, but don't see them in the crowd.

I rush inside, feeling heated, as I look around for where the chaos is going down.

A tall guy, big as all hell, is behind the bar, reaching for bottles of liquor and tossing them at the wall, while Envy and Riley are fighting to stop him from grabbing more.

He swings his elbow back, knocking Envy to the floor and then tosses a bottle of rum at the wall, screaming out as it shatters against the wall.

"Where the fuck is she? I saw her come in here. You're hiding her cheating ass, I know it. Just tell me, bitch. Fuck! Fuck! Brit, where the fuck are you?" His yells are heard even over all the chaos in the room. "I know you're here, bitch."

Adrenaline courses through me as I jump over the bar and grip the back of the giant dick's neck, slamming him face first into the liquor shelf. My momentum makes it easy to turn him toward the bar and throw him into it.

Stopping in front of him, I swing my elbow out hard, connecting it with his jaw when he stands back up. Then I grab the back of his head, slamming it into the side of the bar as hard as I can.

I rotate my shoulders in anger as I look down at him and grip the back of his hair, getting close to the side of his face. "Don't ever fucking come in here again. Touch any of these women or anything else in this club for that matter and I'll rip your fucking throat out."

I feel hands on me trying to pull me off him, but I don't budge until he's forced to see the look in my eyes. I mean fucking business and he better get that before I fuck his ass up even more.

He finally exhales and nods at me. I take this as his surrender and loosen my grip. I take a step back and give him the space he needs to get the fuck out of here.

Standing up, now that I've released his hair, he looks down at the blood on his shirt, before wiping his thumb under his nose and stumbling. "Fuck you, pretty boy. I touch whatever and whoever-"

Before he can finish, Lynx is jumping over the bar himself. Rome is with him and before I know it, they're dragging his ass outside.

Envy reaches for my hand and I pull her to her feet, while fighting to keep my shit under control. He's lucky Lynx and Rome showed up when they did. I'm heated as fuck over this asshole.

"Holy shit, Blaze. I have no idea what happened. He was stumbling over his words and acting like a crazy lunatic. At first he was just breaking beer bottles and then he got behind the bar and kept yelling for Brit, repeatedly, even after we told him that she wasn't here." She's shaking and tears flow down her face as she grips my arm.

I wrap her in my arms, trying to calm her the best I can. "Tell me no one got hurt. You girls all okay?" I pull away from her to watch her expression before she answers.

"Titan took off to grab us all some food, but I managed to keep him distracted enough to make sure no one got hurt. Mostly everyone was out before he got to the point of throwing bottles at the wall."

Holding her tightly again, I look over toward Riley and she gives me a thumbs up while fixing the liquor shelf.

"Where's Brit?" I have to make sure she's safe and I know we'll need to talk to her about her safety after this. He is a maniac and if he goes at her like that, I'm not even sure of the damage he could cause.

Envy shakes her head. "I don't know. She got off over an hour ago and I haven't seen her since. She must've left before he got here."

Lynx and Rome come back a few minutes later, rushing around to check on everyone. It's ladies' night, so this fucker picked the best night to start shit, because there are only a few guys in the bar, all of which are a lot smaller than him.

"Shit, this is not cool at all," Lynx growls out in anger. "We need more security here at night now. I won't take the risk of some asshole doing this again and one of our women or a customer getting hurt."

"Yes," I agree. "The cops take care of that dick?"

Rome looks over from helping Brit with the liquor shelf. "Yeah, the fucker is lucky they got here when they did."

"That asshole could've done a lot more damage if you didn't get here as fast as you did. I would've had to kill his ass if someone got hurt." I listen as Lynx rants and works through the shock that something like this happened. "We need at least two more security guards on every night from now on. The girls are not to be left alone again."

"Consider it done as soon as I leave here."

"Also, get someone set up at Karma's. Now that she's working with us, we'll need to make sure she's set up with the same kind of security our guys are."

I agree with him instantly; in fact, I had already thought of that myself. Even if it comes from my own pocket.

"On it. I'll let you finish up here and I'll get started on increasing security. Let me know if you need me for cleaning or anything else and I'll come back."

I leave with adrenaline coursing through my veins and an urge to relieve some tension one way or another.

My first stop has to be at Karma's, but I quickly make a call to the Alpha House, letting them all know what's happening.

I pass her tattoo shop and notice her car isn't parked there.

I smile remembering the memories of us at her house the last time.

Knocking isn't necessary because she's got the door wide open. I step inside and see her struggling to drag a chair through the living room towards the door that's propped open.

"Let me help with that."

"Damn it, Blaze. You scared the shit out of me." She stands quickly, grabbing her chest. Her red hair falls all around her face, slipping out of the clip she's using to pull it up.

"You really shouldn't leave your door open, you never know when a sex crazed maniac will bust in." She tries not to laugh as I grab the chair from her grasp. "Tell me where it's going."

"I can handle it myself." She's still frustrated with me and I know I'm going to have to fix this quick.

"Quit being so fucking stubborn and let me help you." She exhales and gives in. She has to know I can outlast any stubbornness she can throw my way.

"I'm going to stuff it into the back of my car. I brought it here so I could put it together earlier and now it needs to go to the shop."

I stop walking and turn to look at her.

Is she for real? What woman would do something like that?

"What? I don't have time for that shit when I'm at the shop. My days are insane already. I need to get shit ready for these new artists quickly, so that means I'll be doing a lot of this kind of stuff for a few weeks. Just walk and don't look at me like that."

I can't help but look at her like she's a strange creature that I'm trying to figure out, because that's exactly what I'm trying to do. She's so different from any woman I know and I love that shit about her.

"I didn't say a word, but I'll be putting this in the back of my truck. I'm not sliding this thing inside your car." She's out of her mind for thinking it would fit.

"The last one went in, so this one will too. But if you want to waste time stopping by the shop, that's fine by me."

We start to walk outside and I can feel her eyes on my back. I'm under her skin and she can't help but think about the way I get to her.

"Is this your way of spending more time with me?" She makes me laugh with her straight forward question.

"Hell yes it is. I've never been shy about wanting to spend time with you." If she's going to be straight up, then I will be too.

She smiles as she opens my tailgate and I slide the chair into the bed of my truck. I reach to close the gate, when our hands brush across each other.

Her pause confirms that she's just as interested in me, even if she's frustrated. She may run from me every chance she gets and pretend to not be that attracted to me, but she forgets. I specialize in understanding what women want. It's something I'm very good at, or so I've been told.

Her smile fades and she lowers her head, pulling her lip between her teeth slowly as she looks down my body. I don't miss the catch in her breath as she brushes over my jeans.

My instincts are spot on with her, I'd bet my life on it.

She wants the D and fuck if I don't want to give it to her again.

Chapter FIFTEEN

Karma

HE LOOKS AMAZING AND I want to slide my hands over his firm chest as he watches me. It's truly unfair that he looks as good as he does and he knows it.

If you would've asked me a few days ago if there was another man as good looking as him, I would've told you no. But I've now seen his twin. Double the trouble and sex appeal. These boys are trouble in the best kind of way.

"Why are you looking at me like that?" His deep voice pulls me from my thoughts, causing me to look up at him and see his cocky grin as he watches me check him out.

"I'm not looking at you any way," I lie.

"Is that why you're licking your sexy as fuck lips and fantasizing about my dick?" He's so sure of himself and if he wasn't spot on with what I was doing, I'd put him in his place.

"And what if I am?" I challenge him, knowing it won't take much for him to act on it. To be honest, he's had me rubbing my thighs together many times thinking about how great it felt when he was between them.

He doesn't say a word before he closes in on me, leans down

and throws me over his shoulder. He walks proudly as I try to comprehend how quickly he managed to do that and work not to scream and alert my neighbors.

"Blaze. Stop." My words are quiet and an obvious pathetic attempt to pretend that I don't want him to take me inside and fuck me hard.

"You know you don't want me to stop, but say it again and I will." I take note of his warning and don't leak another word of resistance.

We're barely inside when he slams the front door closed and sets me down in front of it. He moves against me, his blue eyes burning into me as he forces me against the door. I work quickly to pull his shirt up and then he helps me get it over his head in a very sexy way.

How was that so sexy? Because it was Blaze. That's how.

His warm mouth travels over my neck while his hands slide over me hungrily, touching me anywhere and everywhere that he can.

I love how he feels against me. He ignites a fire inside me instantly with his touch and that's something I've struggled with in the past.

"Your skin is flushed. Admit it. I get to you." He smirks as he talks. His confidence is never lacking and maybe that's something I like about him. He knows how to handle a woman and isn't afraid to do it. "You left the house tonight without me showing you what you're leaving." His deep growl against my ear sends chills over my skin and hope through my core that he'll be just as demanding as he always is.

The pressure of his body against mine is so perfectly placed. He lowers himself and unzips my shorts only to run his hands down my legs. "You know these have been driving me crazy since you stepped out of your car at the house. I imagined slipping my finger inside just like this." He slides his fingers between my legs and slips under the material before slowly pushing one finger inside me.

I grab his hair and thrust forward as he enters me, feeling him pull my juices to the surface with each move of that single finger.

That fucking sexy tattooed finger.

"If you're sounding like this with my finger, why have you run from me so many times? My dick will feel so much better, I promise."

I already know how it feels and that's exactly why I've been leaving. He doesn't get to know what he does to me though, so I refuse to respond.

He pulls his finger out, slips my shorts down and then in one swift move he stands with my ass in his hands and glides my back up the door. My legs are over his shoulders and his tongue is buried deep inside me. He steps away from the wall just a little and forces me to wrap myself around him even tighter.

"Fuck." It escapes me in a breathy moan, lingering longer than usual. I run my fingers through his thick hair and grip on tight, holding his face against me.

He moves his head to the side and begins to kiss my inner thigh, lowering me slightly yet holding me in place so he can walk me over to my kitchen bar.

He sets me down carefully before he lowers his head and licks me some more, working his tongue like fucking magic. His touch is so simple, yet exactly what I crave.

"In your room?" He licks me even harder, sucking on my clit until I answer.

"Anywhere is fine . . ." I'm not finished talking before he wraps my legs around his waist and starts walking us to my bed.

He's rough with his kisses and even bites me a few times

once he lays me down. Each time he sends a pleasure through my body, I try to take it in and send myself to the edge.

"Not this time. You have to wait on me this time. I know how you are with that running shit and it isn't happening this time. I'm making sure of it."

I grip the blankets and watch him as he lowers his jeans and takes his dick in his hands. He strokes it a few times, before kicking his jeans aside and spreading my legs wide apart.

Smiling up at him, I reach in the drawer of my nightstand and pull out a condom, keeping my eyes on him, standing there looking so damn sexy.

He watches me with curious eyes as I rip the wrapper open and struggle to roll the condom on his dick. I don't think I've ever struggled with this before.

He laughs as the rubber practically strangles his dick. "It's too small. I have to buy the big ones. Let me get mine." I watch him reach for his jeans and roll one on like he's done it a million times. I quickly shift my focus and try not to think about how many times he's done this.

He moves me up the bed and crawls in between my legs, his body pressing hard against me as he talks directly in my face. "I don't give a shit if the entire world saw that we are fucking. You won't have fuckers in your shop because I'll personally make it my responsibility to handle security. You'll have someone there at all times and I'll even make sure it's a mean fucker that won't put up with a thing." He's so serious that I don't dare argue with him about it. It makes me feel relieved to know that someone will be in there.

I have to admit that I love it when he handles me rough. He does it with such ease that it turns me on to know how strong he is.

Lifting a brow, he squeezes my hands above my head and

slams into me, causing me to scream out from his intrusion. "Now, what were you saying about this being just any old dick?" He thrusts even harder and stops when he's filled me completely. "I guess I need to remind you just what you're referring to." I accept his roughness again and it's that quick that I'm ready to blow.

"You'll quit hiding from the fact that you love how I fuck you. Accept it, just like you accept my dick every time I pound this fucking hungry pussy of yours."

I wrap my legs around his waist and hold him still, while taking a few deep breaths. "Fuck, Blaze. Proving that your dick is big is the last thing you need to do." I grab his hair and yank him down so that I can kiss him. "Getting me to come back for more . . . that's what you need to work on."

I know my words are working him up and that's exactly what I want to do. With Blaze, I like it rough. I want it to hurt so that I believe that it doesn't mean anything more than what it is.

Two people fucking out their frustrations and enjoying each other's bodies.

His mouth and hands are all over my body as he pulls me up to straddle him.

He grinds his hips into me, touching every single spot that makes me go crazy. I can feel every single inch of him this way.

"Is that right?" he questions next to my ear, before thrusting into me hard and then stopping again. "I'll be sure to make you see the benefits of coming around me before I leave then."

With quickness, he flips my body around, remaining between my legs and again slamming into me.

I'm left with the sight of his firm ass and thighs as he buries himself deep inside me and fucks me harder than I've ever been fucked.

"Oh shit . . ." I dig my nails into his strong back and close my eyes, letting his pleasure course through my body.

I meet his thrusts, just for him to pin me down again and bury his face into my neck, biting me.

The mixture of his bite and the way that his dick moves inside me, has me coming undone and there's nothing I can do about.

"Oh shit . . ." I pant. "Blaze . . . Oh . . . Oh . . . fuck."

He continues to move inside my sensitive pussy, pushing me even further over the edge, until I'm coming undone from another orgasm, holding onto him for dear life.

I've never come more than once within in a few minutes with anyone other than him, but the way he moves inside of me, rotating his hips, hits a spot each time that I can't control. He seems to do this, every fucking time we have sex.

He smiles against my lips and stills his hips, giving me a few seconds to catch my breath. "Think you can hold on enough for me to prove that point?" he asks with a cocky smirk.

Turning red with embarrassment, I slap his chest. "Oh, I know I can."

He picks me up and grips my ass, holding me in the air as he pulls out and thrusts back into me over and over again.

His eyes meet mine, so I hold his gaze for as long as I can, before I force myself to turn away the second my heart skips a beat.

I don't think I've ever really noticed how beautiful his eyes were until now.

Dammit, Karma. What the fuck.

Holding on tightly, I dig my nails into his back as he thrusts into me once more, pushing in as deep as he can. I have no choice but to still any movements as he releases his hot come into the condom, not bothering to pull out.

"Holy fuck!" he growls out. "I'm telling you . . ." he smirks.

"Your pussy was made just for me. Not for that asshole ex of yours. If he wants to argue, I'll prove it to him."

"Is that right?" I bounce down on his dick, making him cuss and grip my hair. He's so damn sure of himself. "Oh . . . a little sensitive?"

"Karma . . ." he warns.

Ignoring him, I wrap my arms around his neck and ride him as if my life depends on it.

I ride him hard and fast, biting his bottom lip, until I feel his come filling the condom again.

"Ready to accept that I've proven my point yet?" he pants as I slowly move on him. "Fuck! I love that you're riding my dick like you can't stay off of it."

I smile proudly. "Looks like you're not the only one good at giving orgasms."

Before he gets too comfortable, I slide down his body and start reaching for his clothes. "Get dressed and help me with this damn chair."

Shit . . . did he ever prove his point. Not that he needed to. I was already crazy about what he does to me.

Chapter
SIXTEEN

Blaze

LUCA HAS BEEN WITH THE house for almost a week now and he's pulling in more calls than some of the guys that have been here for months.

It only took him a couple calls to get the hang of it, but he's been blowing it up since then and loving it.

Lynx thought it'd be a good idea to throw another mansion party and show Luca the crazy shit that goes down around here. He hasn't had his proper welcoming yet.

We're just waiting on Luca to come up with a theme so we can get the invitations out.

"Holy fuck," Luca pops his head into my room, sounding out of breath. "This is insane. I get to invite any ten girls that I want this weekend?"

I take a minute to finally look at Luca to see that he's running around in a pair of briefs, still hard from his last show. "You haven't worked that shit out yet, bro?" I laugh as he pushes down on his erection and walks farther into my room.

"Only fucking five times so far today." He holds up his right hand as if he has a cramp. "Shit. I'm not as good with my left. I'm gonna need more practice."

"I heard you already got asked to do a call with Rome. You comfortable jerking off next to another dude?"

I look my twin over and can see where we're different. I'll jerk my shit anywhere in front of anyone. I'm not ashamed.

He looks hesitant, but quickly covers it up with a smartass remark just like I would.

"And show him up with my huge cock." He walks over and grabs my favorite pair of jeans from the pile of clothes that I still haven't put away yet. "Looks like we have the same taste in more than just women. I'll be borrowing these."

"Yeah, but those jeans will be the only thing you're borrowing, brother. So enjoy, fucker." I stand up as he slips into my jeans. "They look good on us."

"I know, right? They really accentuate the important things in life. I think I'll wear these for my last call tonight."

"Don't jerk your dick in my jeans!" I yell after him as he takes off in my expensive ass jeans. The dick is lucky he's my twin and that the jeans look good on him. Or else I'd take the fuckers back.

When I get downstairs, Levi and Nash are both doing calls, but in separate rooms.

Levi has one hand down the front of his low hanging jeans, talking dirty to one of his callers. He nods at me as I pass, then goes right back to taking demands from his caller.

Nash tilts his hat at me from the kitchen, while holding his damn dick in the other as I pass by.

The things these women request to see never seem to surprise me.

I've been asked to do my show in the kitchen plenty of times because the women think having a man in the kitchen is extremely hot and a turn on.

Some women just like the idea of the living room and other random places in the house, because it's a public fucking show. Public sells.

They like the idea that other Alphas are walking around the house possibly catching glimpses of their call. It's a turn on to them.

When I walk out back, Rome is sitting in front of his laptop looking stressed the fuck out.

"What's up, man? Everything good?"

He looks up at me, while pulling his hair back and I can see just how tired he is. "I'm good. Just overbooked for the week and my dumbass had the bright idea of taking on more clients. I haven't slept in over thirty hours and haven't had pussy in over ten days."

"Let me know if you need any rescheduled and Rebel can take care of it. Don't break your dick trying to take on every request." I smile knowing he's looking burnt out and needs a little encouragement. We've all been there. "You need that shit. You're one of the top demands of the Alpha House right now. Don't let me down, fucker."

He closes down his laptop. "Nah, I'm good. I have a few hours before my next call. I'm getting my dick some much needed action and then crashing the hell out while I can."

"Sounds like a good idea, man. Gotta break in some of those toys and shit."

I hear a car pull up and Rome moves quickly. "There's my pussy call. Talk to you later, brother." He moves in a hurry and I know not to hold him back.

His urgency has me thinking of my own. A week is a long fucking time for me. I don't have a call for another two hours so I decide to pay Karma a surprise visit.

Charlie greets me when I get to the shop and then watches

me with a humorous smile as I let myself into Karma's room without asking.

It takes a few seconds for Karma to realize that I'm here. She's working a piece on some dude's thigh.

"Do I need to start locking my door?" she questions with a small smile that she's trying to hide. "I don't need any distractions right now, Blaze. I'm sorta busy as you can see. It's called knocking. Do it next time."

I take a seat on a stool and flash her a sexy grin, knowing that it'll soften her up a bit. "Hey, I can't help it if my good looks are a distraction." She looks up at me. "Don't watch me. I'm just gonna sit back here and look good and try not to stroke my cock to watching you tattoo, looking sexy as fuck as you concentrate."

She growls and shakes her head. "Dammit, Blaze. Don't fuck with me. This is a first timer. I need to make a good impression."

The client doesn't even know I'm here because he's rocking out with some headphones on, facing the other direction.

"You're sexy as hell with that tattoo gun in your hand. When are you going to tat me up, naked?"

She clenches her jaw and pretends that my words aren't affecting her, but I can tell by her breathing that I'm working her up.

"We can see how good you can tattoo through an orgasm as my dick is buried in that sweet little pussy, filling you."

"Blaze!" She shoots me a hard look and then goes back to trying to concentrate on her tattoo, but she can't seem to keep her eyes off of me. "One more word and I'll tattoo your dick in your sleep."

"You'll have a lot of canvas then."

"Don't you have a call to take or something? I'm busy, Blaze."

I stand up and walk around, Karma's eyes instantly zoning

in on my obvious erection.

"Not for a couple of hours." I grab my dick and rub it through my jeans. "Need my help with anything? I'll be glad to help."

"You just never stop, do you?" She laughs.

"I can stop . . . if you want me to."

Her eyes look up to lock on mine, but she quickly looks back down.

She doesn't respond to that, so I sit back down and watch her in silence, until she's done with her client.

After she sends him off to find Charlie at the desk, she walks back into the room and shuts the door behind her.

Before she can say anything, I grip her hips and back her up against the wall. "I want you to be my guest at the party this weekend." I squeeze her hips and grin. "I can show you all of the rooms that we're going to fuck in."

"I bet you'd love that." Her hand slides down the front of my body, stopping on my dick. "Maybe I'm busy this weekend."

I look down at her hand and then back up at her with a cocky grin. "I could show you now. Keep testing me. I'll throw you over my shoulder and carry your ass out of here."

"Uhh . . . Karma." Charlie opens the door and pokes her head in. "Your next client is here."

"Give me two minutes and then send them in." She presses her hands against my chest and pushes me away. "I'm cleaning up now."

"Got it, boss." Charlie winks at me and disappears. Even she can see how much Karma wants my dick right now.

I watch Karma as she walks away and starts preparing for her next client. She wants to play it off as if she doesn't want to come this weekend, but fuck that shit. Her games won't work on me.

"See you this weekend. I'll send your official invitation tonight."

I open the door and she turns around to look at me. "And if I don't accept?"

"You will." I wink and let myself out, leaving her worked up and most likely thinking about all the things I'll do to her this weekend.

After the way she grabbed my dick . . . I'll be surprised if she can wait 'til this weekend.

Chapter
SEVENTEEN

Karma

AFTER BLAZE LEFT, MY CONCENTRATION was shit. All I could think about was wanting to rip those jeans down his thighs and tattooing his beautiful body.

The idea of tattooing, naked, has never sounded so damn appealing until I pictured doing it with him.

He knew that stopping in here would get my mind on him and it worked. He got what he wanted, because I'm half tempted to show up at the house tonight and let him see what it feels like to be distracted from work.

"You taking off early?" Charlie asks with a grin, while watching me clean up.

"Why would I?"

"Oh don't play stupid. You've been talking about Blaze and his call that should be happening any minute, ever since he walked out that damn door."

"I have one more client tonight. I can't just leave." I point out the obvious and try to pretend I'm not thinking about him.

"Actually, your last client just canceled. So . . . yeah you can. Go and show this Blaze guy that two can play. You're done here.

I can take care of the rest. There's enough hot security outside to help me if I need it. I'm liking this new setup." She grins.

I have to turn away quickly because I can't help but to smile when I think of the ways that I can torment him while he works. The thought has me feeling ecstatic as I finish cleaning up my work room and prepare for tomorrow.

He's so damn confident. I've never found that so attractive on a man before. Normally, I want to knock them down a level, but with him, he just knows how to get to me. He has the confidence, but I can feel that he's so much more than all of that. His persistence is getting to me.

"I'll see you tomorrow. Lock up for me after all the artists finish up." I keep walking toward the door and avoid looking at Charlie. I know she's grinning like a complete idiot because she likes how Blaze gets to me and because well . . . the hot security just within her reach.

"This is all taken care of. You go get you some from that fine ass twin." Her laughter is obnoxious, but I have to love her. We tend to live vicariously through each other here at the shop. It keeps things entertaining.

My drive to the Alpha House is short and not long enough for me to have a real plan of distraction when I hit the door. Looks like I'll have to wing it.

I know how he is and it won't take much at all for him to drop everything with his clients and fuck me right in the very room I begin to torment him in.

I can hear laughter near the pool when I open my car door. It's definitely Blaze's voice yelling over the music and at least two others talking to him.

Am I ready for this?

Do I want to take this step toward him, no doubt opening up a whole new set of rules in whatever this set up is the two of us have?

I have tried to stay clear of him since that first night we hooked up, but he's persistent as hell and I can slowly feel my walls crumbling around him. I'm enjoying his company a lot more than I'd hoped to.

I open the gate and he's instantly headed toward me, barely giving me a chance to take a step inside it.

"Fuck yeah. I knew you couldn't stay away." His excitement is apparent in his voice and in the way he wraps me up in his arms the second he's near.

"You're dripping wet!" He picks me up and starts to carry me toward the pool where the other guys are hollering obscenities at us. My legs are again wrapped around his waist and he's walking with me like this is just what we do.

"I never judge you when you're soaked." His deep whisper is barely heard over the splashing behind me, but it's enough to send goose bumps over my flesh.

"Ah shit. Are you about to drop me some fucking sweetness in this pool?" I think that's Levi's voice behind me, but I never really get the chance to look because Blaze keeps walking past them all and into the house before he sets me on my own two feet.

"You know . . . I can actually walk on my own in case you haven't noticed." I point to his chest in a teasing manner just before he pulls my hips toward his. He holds me close and just looks into my eyes for a few seconds before he finally starts to talk.

"Oh, I've noticed your walk. In fact, if you don't mind not walking in front of the other guys in the house, that would be perfect." He leans forward to give me a quick peck on the lips before he reaches around me for another beer. "Here. You're a few behind, so I'll let you get caught up while I finish my calls. Next one starts in five minutes. I'll even let you watch if you promise to tease the fuck out of me while I'm working."

How can he even want me to do that? My plan to torment him is busted and in fact it's actually what he wants from me.

Fucking Blaze . . .

"You would like that wouldn't you? How about I just hang out by the pool and you can just come down when you're finished." He looks at me with a disappointed look in his eye, but I know he'll finagle something to his benefit before this is all said and done.

"I'll take that beer and wait for you outside," I say while reaching for the cold beer in his hand and leaving him standing by himself to watch my ass as on the way out the door.

I feel his eyes on my back even when I'm walking outside. I have no doubt that he's thinking up ways for things to work out for his benefit.

Levi is getting out of the pool, leaving only Luca in the water, as I walk up. Levi winks at me, but doesn't say a word as he walks past me and into the house.

"My brother is truly trying to test me." Luca's deep laugh echoes across the water and I have to swallow hard to continue walking. I can handle these guys, I mean hell, I own a tattoo shop and have to deal with worse than all of them daily and never have an issue holding my own.

"Nothing to test," I say with a small smile. "Plus, I'm pretty sure he'll be out here soon himself." After everything I've been through with Blaze, I honestly couldn't see myself even attempting to be with one of the other guys in the house. Not even his damn twin and they're just alike.

Rome walked up to the pool a few seconds ago, but silently goes inside. I'm not sure what he's thinking about, but he looks exhausted.

"I'm sure you're correct. That red hair of yours is probably making him a little crazy. He's always liked playing with fire. In fact, I used to call his ass Pyro." I walk slowly to the nearest lounge chair and sit on the side, watching the moonlight reflect off of the water.

"I could see that. He seems like he loves a good challenge." I swallow a drink of my beer, knowing that's exactly what I am. A fucking challenge. That's why I'm still single. No one has tried as hard as Blaze has. Honestly, no one has been able to quite handle me.

"He does. Until he conquers it. Then he tends to get a little bored. So if I were you, I'd keep up what you're doing. Keep him chasing, because honestly . . . he hasn't found one worth chasing for some time." I try to decide if he's trying to scare me off or truly help me. Whatever it is, I don't like this feeling that is creeping up on me, thinking about Blaze getting bored with me.

"Is this your way of running me off?" I stare him down, trying to read him.

He laughs even louder as he runs his hand over his long hair and then dips into the pool before coming back up and shaking the water off .

"Hell no. My brother hasn't called shotgun in forever. I'm enjoying the fuck out of watching him get all weird with you. That smooth ass isn't so smooth when he has to deal with all the emotional crap. Makes me feel like I still have game left when he's off like this." He pushes up on the side of the pool and slides out.

"I'm sure you have plenty of your own game."

With looks like that. I mean he is a spitting image of Blaze, so I'm allowed to appreciate him for that reason alone. They even share some of the same tattoos, Luca just has a few more than Blaze does. *For now anyway.*

"I do alright." He starts to use a towel to dry off and I make myself look into the water. It's so easy to get distracted with him because of their similarities.

"I'm supposed to choose the next house party theme. I can't seem to decide. Do you think a masquerade party or a Vegas themed party would be more fun?"

I begin to think of the scenario for both and know that both would be a blast in this house. *As long as Blaze is here.*

I pull myself from my thoughts of Blaze and respond to Luca. "You really can't go wrong with either."

I take another drink when I see Blaze rushing through the kitchen. He has his phone in his hand and he's obviously live on a call. *And oh my god, he's coming outside.*

Luca leaves the instant Blaze hits the door and I watch with a giant smile on my face as he begins to show off to his caller, all the while watching me over the phone.

He's teasing me as I sit here and I have to ask myself, do I feel like it's play time, or do I just sit back and enjoy the show for tonight.

Because if there's one thing I know, Blaze knows how to put on a great fucking show!

Chapter

EIGHTEEN

Blaze

KARMA MUST BE CRAZY AS hell if she thought I'd leave her ass outside by the pool, knowing that my brother and Levi were out here.

Well . . . they're definitely not out here anymore because the fuckers knew they'd get an eyeful of cock if they stuck around.

My caller is talking, but my eyes have been glued to Karma, watching me from the lounge chair, looking sexy as all hell.

Her legs are spread open, one hand trailing up the inside of her thigh, as she holds the beer to her lips and tilts it back all sexy like.

"She slides the top of the bottle in her mouth and teases my cock with the thought of her mouth on me like that.

A little smirk crosses her face when my caller has to repeat herself. She's distracting my ass and she knows exactly what she's doing.

" . . . can you hear me over the water? Blaze . . ."

I pull my eyes away from Karma and look at *Hot2Nite* on the screen. She's one of my few callers that shows her face and probably one of the hottest too.

Long blonde hair. Insanely sexy green eyes and tits that fill up most of the screen. I used to look forward to her calls . . . until Karma started to consume me.

I lift a brow and walk into the water, setting the phone up on the stand so that the caller can see me without me holding it and I still have a perfect view of Karma and anything she decides to do. I'm against the edge of the pool closest to Karma, so she can't see unless I step away from the side.

"You want me in the water . . ." I duck into the water and run my hands over my wet hair. I emerge from the water, dripping wet and try to focus on the caller. "I'm wet just like you fucking want."

"Holy. Fuck. Yes, you are. I am too now, Blaze. You're always so quick to get me wet." Her attempt at sexy talk does nothing for me with Karma in the background.

My eyes go up to get a glimpse of the most distracting woman I've ever met. She has this little crooked smile on her lips, as she sits up and slowly strips down to her matching black bra and panties.

Then she nods as if she's telling me to continue.

When I look back down at my phone, it's hard to tell from this tiny screen, but it looks like my caller has also stripped down to just a bra.

"Well, fuck," I mutter to myself, before talking loud enough to be heard. "Is someone getting naked so it's easier to finger fuck?"

Karma gives me a mischievous look, as she stands up and walks toward the pool. Keeping her eyes on me, she pours the beer between her breasts and then runs her hands down the front of her body.

"Fuck me . . ." My eyes stay glued to Karma as I reach for my hard cock and begin stroking it.

"There we go. Yes, Blaze," my caller thinks that I'm stroking myself for her, but she's so fucking wrong.

"Sit on the edge of the pool so I can see you touching yourself. Show me that big, beautiful cock of yours that I love so much."

I jump up onto the tiled edge of the pool and grab my shaft with both hands, slowly stroking it as I watch Karma slip her hand into the front of her underwear and slide it in and out. I have to work to stay on camera on fight the urge of just going straight to Karma and handling business.

"Take it out of your boxers, Blaze. I only have five minutes' left. I'm so close," my caller moans in desperation. "I need this."

I hear Karma suck in a breath as she watches me pull my erection free from my boxers and slowly run my hands up and down it. My dramatic moan gets to them both, just like I knew it would.

"Oh fuck! Oh . . . fuuuuck!" I don't even bother looking down at the phone when my caller gets off, like I usually would with this one.

I don't even care that my caller is still online, I slide my boxers off completely and pull Karma into the pool with me. Instantly my hands are gripping her hair and the sexy as fuck breath she takes encourages me to pull her head back so I can talk against her.

"I should fuck you right now," I breathe into her neck, before slowly biting it. "But the other dicks in this house will come running as soon as they hear you scream, wanting to get a view of you being *fucked*."

She wraps her legs around my waist, teasing me, by grinding her pussy against my cock. "You afraid one of them might want to join?"

"Woah . . . is this something I can pay to see now?" We both look at my phone when my caller speaks.

"Maybe someday," I say with a smirk. "Not today, babe."

Her call will end within a minute anyway, so I pretend that she's not even there and go back to focusing on Karma.

Actually, yeah. I am afraid that one of these assholes would try to join and I have a feeling that just so Karma can keep me at a distance that she would agree to it.

Fuck that shit . . .

"I wouldn't let that shit happen." I reach down and grab her pussy as if I own it. "I'm the only one getting inside this sweet pussy and making you come *over* and *over* again . . ."

"Is that right?" she challenges, while grinding against me. "What makes you think that you have a say?"

Grinning, I slip my finger inside her and begin sliding it in and out as I talk. "Because as much as you play it off, Karma," I push in hard, making her moan out, "you want me around and inside of you." I slide in another finger and push in as deep as I can. "Like I said . . . your pussy was made just for me and you know it too."

"I made a decision on the party theme. A fucking masquerade party. My ass looks fly in a suit." Luca surprises us both just before he jumps into the water and swims close to us.

Just to fuck with Karma, I continue to finger fuck her under the water, while she fights to act normal as if nothing's going on.

"Oh yeah . . ." I look up at Luca and grin. "We do look good in a suit, brother."

I turn to Karma and brush my lips against hers, catching her moan as I relentlessly finger fuck her. "And I bet you'd look fine as fuck in masquerade attire. I can help you pick out a dress if you want. After all . . . I'll be the one ripping it off you later."

Karma digs her nails into my back before she wraps her arms around my shoulders and raises out of the water and starts to ride my hand, sending her into her orgasm.

She finishes by biting my shoulder and melts against me as she comes undone in my arms. She tries to hide her moans, but fails miserably when I curl my finger and take her all the way through the end of a great release.

My tongue craves the curve of her breasts, but I hold back knowing I don't want to go there with an audience. I'm not sure I could keep her covered if I went any further. Once I get started with her, it kills me to pull back. He's already seen more of her than I wanted. He didn't get to see her naked, but I know he didn't turn away from watching her orgasm just now. Watching her come is something I'll never get tired of, but not anything I plan to share again.

One of these days I'm going to have to lock us in a room and spend some quality time with her to accomplish what I truly want to do to her.

Luca lifts a brow, smirking once he realizes what he just walked into. "I always have the perfect timing, brother."

Karma pushes away from me and swims toward the edge of the pool.

I watch as she climbs out and walks over to grab her clothes. Once she's done gathering them, she looks down and me and Luca. "I guess I'll see you boys this weekend." Her eyes lock on mine. "I'll be looking for my invitation."

With that, she walks away, half-naked and dripping wet, not giving a shit who might see her running around in her underwear.

"Damn, brother. I almost want to kick your ass for calling shotgun."

I turn to him and smile. "I'd like to see you try, fucker." I pull myself out of the water and look down at Luca. "She's worth the fight."

Luca gives me a knowing smile. "I can tell. You look at her

differently than I've ever seen you look at a girl. It's almost scary."

"And she's the only girl I'm fucking right now, so that should tell you everything you need to know."

Luca leans his elbows on the side of the pool before he replies to me. "So is it official, or just an unspoken fuck buddy relationship the two of you have?"

I don't like how his words hit me, but it's not his fault. I'm not one to jump into relationships, and I can tell she isn't either.

Honestly, if I had pushed any harder than I have, I'm pretty sure she would've run for the fucking hills. Her adamant attempts to keep me away haven't stopped me, but I do know when to push and when not to.

"Guess it's an unofficial deal, but in my eyes, it's official. I'll have to work on her a little to get past that fucking wall of hers." I slide out of the pool and decide I need to do something epic with this hard on I'm sporting. And I think since it's her fault, she gets to help.

"Looks to me like you've got a magic pass through that wall, brother. Can you please put that fucker away?" I stand and walk toward the towels, leaving him with a view of my ass. He needs to learn not to come near me when Karma's around if he doesn't want a fucking show.

"Yeah well, it's your damn fault I still have this fucker. How 'bout the next time you see us in the pool together, you turn and walk the fuck away. Or I'll position myself so that you just see my ass as I handle my business."

He knows I'm not kidding in the slightest, in fact the past proves that I don't give a fuck where I'm naked and who the fuck sees me fucking.

The only thing that's changed is, I don't want anyone to see her gorgeous fucking body.

Chapter
NINETEEN

Karma

I NEED A HOT SHOWER now. Damn Blaze and the way he can make me come undone like I'm an inexperienced teenager.

The way he talks to me, so deep and demanding just sends me straight onto the edge and ready for anything with him.

I step into the shower and let the hot water remind me of his touch. I can still feel his fingers deep inside me, pulling out every emotion in me. He's so bossy and normally that would infuriate me, yet with him I find myself instantly agreeing to do whatever he demands. At least my body does.

The doorbell rings just as I begin drying off. I toss my hair into a towel and then wrap another around my body to go see who is here.

It's late and I refuse to open the door in my towel, so I look through the peep hole and smile the second I see Blaze's face shining in the light.

I can't deny that the sight of him made my heart skip a beat.

Turning the knob, I step behind the door and let him in. He closes the door instantly and without a word pulls the towel from my hair before he tugs the other one loose, letting them both fall to my feet.

"Quit fucking leaving before I'm finished with you. It makes me more aggressive when I have to chase your ass around."

He pulls my hair in a tight grip and leans in to kiss my neck. "Here's your damn invitation. I want you," he nibbles and kisses up my neck and around my ear, "to come to that fucking party with me this weekend. Wear a dress you don't love because I plan to rip the thing right off your body, just like I said." He bites down on my neck before he continues.

"Be ready to stay the fucking night. You'll be sleeping with me, that is, if we fucking sleep." He pulls me closer, gripping my ass in both hands and grinding me closer to his hips. The obvious erection he has is probably the reason he rushed over here in the first place.

I reach between us and grip him tight. It's time he learns to listen as well as he demands. "Prepare yourself, Blaze. Because I plan to be at that party. And I actually enjoy all-nighters with a promise of sex. Let's just see if you can handle it." My grip tightens and he moans into my mouth.

"I'm about to pin you up against this door and fuck you hard, just like your body is begging for." He grinds forward into me before he leans us both into the door, gripping my ass with his free hand

"What makes you so sure I'm craving you?"

He dips his fingers between my legs and draws even more moisture from me. "Because you're already ready for me and I just got here." He removes his fingers, leaving me once again empty before he takes them both into his mouth. "Or is this you still remembering me in the pool? Either way, you want me."

He steps away from me, only to watch me try to compose myself, I'm sure. And just that quick, I'm ready to wrap my legs around his waist and let him take me to pound town.

"It's time I seal the deal on this fucking invitation proper-ly. Where do you want me to fuck you? I'll even let you choose since that seems to be what we do at your house." He holds his arms out and looks around my front living room. I'm still stand-ing naked, watching him from against the door and missing his body against mine.

I choose to use my best assets to make him stop talking and start doing. Walking by him, I walk proudly up the stairs and into my bedroom.

Reaching for my brush, I start moving it through my hair while he watches closely. It takes him only a few seconds before he's gripping his cock through his jeans and walking even closer to me.

He reaches for my brush and takes over. I stand there some-what awkwardly letting him get the rest of the tangles out, be-fore he once again grips it all into one hand and pulls my head back slightly.

Fuck, I love my hair being pulled and I'm sure the sound of my exhale tells him just that.

"Alright, against the window it is. Let the world watch me invite you to my fucking party." The sound of his zipper and the wrapper of the condom make me excited and I almost don't even think about him smashing my tits against the window as he starts to enter me.

This window is a floor to ceiling window that faces away from the other houses. I'm not worried about anyone seeing us, unless someone is out walking this late.

He thrusts forward, gripping my hips so tight, I'll no doubt have marks from his fingers. "You've been invited, so now I need a response. Fucking tell me yes every time I enter you just so I know you're excited to come to the Alpha House just for me." His thrust is hard and his grip even tighter.

"Yessss." I'll say it a thousand times if he enters me like this. He does it again, even harder, and I don't say anything just to see what he does.

He stops moving, only to allow his words to seduce me again. A bite to my shoulder leads his threat. "I told you to fucking say yes every time I enter you. Do it again and I stop. Now fucking say yes."

"Yessss," I moan out. Oh my god he's so rough and every time he moves into me, my tits hit the cold window, making me feel so many different sensations across my body.

The bite mark still stinging from before sits right next to the new spot he chooses to bite. Fuck me. "Yessss." He thrusts again.

He's slowly torturing me and I love every minute of it. His grip changes and he takes a step back, before he begins moving me onto him instead of him thrusting into me.

"Fuck yes, Karma. You feel so good on my cock."

"Yes." I continue to say it every time he hits me deep. My nipples still barely touching the window each time he moves me forward. My back is arched and I'm on my tip toes trying to make every single move perfect.

"Fuck. I'm about to come, you're so damn perfect." He runs his hands up my back before he grips my shoulders and starts to fuck me so fast and hard I don't have time to say yes until my release runs all over me.

I can feel his grip all over me even when we both stop moving. Our breathing is erratic and a perfect reflection of what we just went through. He doesn't release me from his hold and I don't try to leave.

Why does he make me feel so good? No other man has ever been able to accomplish this every time we're together, yet he's still managing to do it.

"Don't take this as a sign of what you have to look forward to Saturday night. This is just me getting started. I can fuck all damn day and all night." He slides his hands down my side and back over my chest, pinching my nipples before he brushes the rest of my chest with his touch.

"I'll hold you to it," I whisper against his cheek and relish in his touch even further. I find myself looking forward to this party now more than ever. I never thought I'd be this into someone like Blaze, but I guess I never really took the whole package into consideration.

He's proven how smart he is and that he's willing to stand up for me. Hell, he hasn't given up trying to get me into his bed no matter how many times I've rejected him. I know men like him don't have to chase pussy, so I know this is a big deal for him. I'm not an idiot, I just have to decide how much of him I'm going to allow into my life.

I can tell if he had it how he wanted, he'd be with me every single day and that's something I know I'm not ready for.

He slides his hands over my clit and starts circling it with the perfect amount of pressure, again bringing me to a release quickly with his dick still twitching inside me. I moan through another orgasm at his fingertips, while I can hear the smile on his face as he talks to me.

"So easy to get to you Karma. I can't wait to see how many times I can make you come in one night. The magic number is three so far. That's not enough when it comes to you."

I guess instead of over thinking the two of us, I should just have fun along the way.

There's no doubt with this man and his dick, I'm going to have a ton of fun.

Chapter
TWENTY

Blaze

THE HOUSE IS FULL OF pussy, yet none I want to even spend a minute getting to know. I'm impatiently waiting for Karma to get here and it's almost embarrassing how excited I am to see her again.

There are so many women walking around in dresses, all of them with their faces mostly covered. I know she's not here, because I haven't seen her fire red hair yet. Not to mention her walk is one I'll recognize the second she enters the door.

I'm sitting at the bar on the second floor watching them all enter. Rome begins to pour the shots and Luca just looks in awe at all the possibilities literally at his feet.

"This is absolute insanity. How many threesomes have you had in this house? I'm starting with number one tonight for damn sure."

My mind goes back to the only one that almost happened and I quickly change the subject. Shit, my brother is going to think I've lost my game when in fact, I've just simply changed it up a bit.

"What? Are you already trying to decide which two you're

taking to your room? So fucking sure of yourself." I have to give him hell or it wouldn't be a normal conversation between two twin brothers.

"Nah brother, not yet, just licking my lips knowing I'm not tied down to one pussy tonight. Oh shit, I'm gonna fuckin' love this house."

"Drink up, pussies. You'll all be in line behind me tonight." Rome hands us a shot and we all drink it quickly and set it down for him to pour again.

"Is Lynx in the house tonight?" I haven't even talked to him today so I don't know what his plans will be. I figured if anything, Rome would know.

"Yes, he'll be here with Rebel before the night is over," he responds.

Lynx has locked his bedroom door and I figured he'd be using it on party nights. He's not ready to pull away completely, but he has stopped doing calls all together. He has enough work in just running the business matters with Rebel.

"It's nice to see those two shackin' up. Lynx isn't quite the asshole he was without her." I stop talking to Luca when another group of girls walk in.

I try to hide my disappointment when none of them are her. She's fucking with me and working me up by making me wait. I'm growing impatient the longer I have to wait.

"Looking for that firecracker of yours?" Luca reaches for another shot and turns to wait for a reply from me.

"Yeah, she'll be here shortly."

"Do I get another show? If so, could you not cover her up so fucking much?" I let him tease me because she's not here, but if it came down to it, I'd never let him see her like that again.

"Looks like she'll be doing a piece on my leg soon for one of her shows." He surprises me with that bit of information.

"Really. When did this happen?" I can't pretend that this doesn't irritate me. I don't like the idea of them making plans behind my back.

"She called today asking, so I told her yes." He so confidently takes a drink while I swallow nothing and try to not be an idiot about this.

"I asked her why she's not doing yours live, and she said something about doing yours the week before mine."

I sit back with a little bit of anticipation running through my mind. She *will* be tattooing me naked, so it's just as well that it's not on live feed.

The door opens once again and she walks in. I can tell it's her the instant the door opens. Confidence radiates from her every move and my dick is already twitching with the thought of her being here.

"Fuck. That woman is ridiculous. You're a lucky bastard." Rome's grumble makes me laugh.

I love the respect we all have for each other and the code we all accept when it comes to standing back when one of us is really interested in a woman. Things in this house would get messy as fuck if one of us didn't.

I walk slowly down the stairs to meet her. She looks around the room until she sees me approaching her and it warms me to feel her instantly wrap her arms around me in a greeting.

"You look sexy as fuck. I'm so glad you wore this dress." I can see her full cleavage, and the back is completely open with tiny straps holding it in place. It hugs her curves perfectly and shows off many of her tattoos. I couldn't have designed this better if I wanted. It's like it was made for her specifically.

Before she can respond to me, Lynx's deep voice fills the room, drawing the attention of the whole room. I missed them coming in. He must've come in from the back.

"Alright. I need your attention to the main stage. It's time we line up some of our most cherished callers for a special treat tonight. It's time for body shots and there's only one way to do those according to Rebel." Lynx smiles at his girlfriend and I get excited knowing I'm about to get a little taste of Karma, and this time it won't be the world paying me back for the bad shit I've done in the past.

It's a new type of Karma that I'm cursed with and it's a sentence I'm fucking excited to see through to the end.

"Looks like it's time to show those two how this is really done. You up for a show?" She smiles and accepts my hand as I find myself again walking her to the front of an audience for a little tease.

The women begin yelling her name before we even get to the stage. Looks like she has a fan base already from just a single show in the house. That's good news for both businesses.

"Rome, Luca, Levi . . . get your asses down here." Lynx calls for all of the guys who aren't already down here. The crowd of girls move forward in hopes of being one of the lucky ones. I watch each of the guys pick a woman and smile at the variety we have up here.

We are here to entertain all women, so it's perfect that we have a diverse group of callers each time we do something like this.

But I'll only be doing this with Karma. She's mine for the night and every night I can get her to come in this house. She gets my attention first and honestly even if I tried to divert it from her, my mind wouldn't allow it.

She stands next to me and I can feel her slight stress now that we're in front of everyone again. I decide to get this started and ease her mind and stop any issues she's starting to imagine in that gorgeous head of hers.

"Should I go first?" I whisper in her ear and watch her move for the shot glasses that are already filled with tequila.

"I'm first. Keep your hands back and let me do this." She removes her mask and then removes mine. Her smile is naughty and I can't wait to see what she's about to do.

"Looks like Karma has decided that ladies will go first. Ladies, prepare your shots and don't disappoint those who are stuck watching this." Lynx hands the mic to one of our bartenders and I see Rebel guide Lynx against the wall before Karma moves me toward the back.

"On your back." She runs her fingers down my chest and over the ridges of my stomach, while looking me in the eye with confidence.

"You want me on the ground?" I'm honestly distracted by her so I'm not sure if she's going to do a shot off my back or if she wants me lying on it.

"Did I fucking stutter? Get on your back and prepare yourself for a shot you'll never forget." I have no choice but to follow her lead now. She's intriguing the hell out of me and I love the tease in the air between us.

I lie on my back and smile as she steps over me. She's not wearing any panties and I can't wait to torment her for this little show she's giving me.

"Who wants to see me unzip his pants? Use that big cock as a chaser for this tequila?" She yells over the women already screaming for a show and instantly the room erupts in approval of her idea.

She has obviously lost any reservations of keeping us on a professional level in the public eye. If she actually pulls my cock out as a chaser, it will be her claiming me in a way. These women like a man who's single, so this will be interesting to see how it all plays out.

This is actually overstepping all of the house rules when it comes to being out in the open at these parties, but who the fuck am I to enforce a dumb rule when I've got the view I have up her dress right now?

I can't wait to see if she's really going to do this in front of everyone.

Fuck the rules. Fuck all the rules in the ass, because there's no way in hell I'm stopping her.

Chapter TWENTY ONE

Karma

HOLY SHIT, WHAT HAVE I done? Knowing this hot as fuck man is mine for the night has made me a little bold in front of this crowd.

When I heard most of them yelling my name as he brought me forward, I knew I had to be bold up here, just like I was in my show. It's something that will sell my show and I may as well tease him while I send an increase in my viewership.

He set us up as an obvious fucking couple on that first show, so it's not like I'm revealing anything with what I'm about to do.

I'm standing over him with no panties on and I know it's driving him crazy. I didn't miss his groan when he got the first view.

I let the crowd make the decision, knowing what their answer would be. I guess I get to sort of mark my territory with this shot. If viewers didn't pick up on our chemistry before, they will tonight.

Dropping to my knees, I straddle his face and let my dress

fall around me. Just like I knew he would, he starts licking me so perfectly and I have to work to seem unaffected by his tongue moving all around my already wet pussy. The thought of all of this has me ready for anything with him.

He doesn't move a muscle that's obvious to those watching. As far as they all know I'm sitting on his face with my panties creating a barrier between us. *Holy fuck is that not the case.*

I lean forward and unzip his pants, then sit proudly, straddling his face. Luca smiles hugely as he hands me my shot glass and I give him a grin right back, knowing that he's probably the only one who knows what's going on under my dress right now.

Call this payback for the pool scene.

I lean over his body and lick the ridges of muscle on his stomach, following the perfect 'V' to the edge of his pants. Teasing him just enough to see his dick throbbing underneath the thin fabric. I purposely don't pull out his cock, not wanting it out on complete display.

Shifting my hips just slightly, I sit back upright and move even closer to his mouth, allowing a nibble just as I lean my head back and take the shot.

Without hesitation I reach for his zipper and slide forward, pulling his cock out and sliding it in my mouth only once before I tuck it back inside his pants and out of sight.

The room is insanely loud right now, but it's all just noise to me as I try to maintain composure while he is making me crazy with his tongue.

Knowing I need to move very soon, I take Luca's hand and stand to adjust my dress and steady myself on these hooker heels I decided to wear tonight.

The look on Blaze's face is priceless and the hunger is obvious on his face. He rubs his palm over his beard, smiling like an idiot and running his tongue over his lower lip. This is just the beginning of an insane night and I just set the pace.

"Best chaser possible. No lies," Luca says close to my ear. "But doesn't look like I needed to tell you that. My brother is one lucky fucker."

I don't know what to say to him except "thank you".

Looking cocky as hell, Blaze rises to his feet and pushes down on his erection, while looking straight at me.

He's letting me know with the curve of his mouth, that he liked what I just did to him, and that he's ready to retaliate for that little show.

This may be a long night of back and forth teasing until one of us gives in. It's usually me, I don't think Blaze is ever done to be honest.

Meeting his gaze, I run my tongue over my lips, making sure to lick up every spilt drop.

Then we both look over at Luca as he picks two women from the crowd, nodding for us to watch him do the shots on two sets of tits that make mine look small.

Smiling, I look back at Blaze before walking away, knowing damn well that he'll be quick to chase me after the taste I just gave him.

I don't even get fifteen feet away, before I feel his grip around my waist, him slamming me hard against his body. "Dance with me," he demands. "You got up before I could make you come."

Pulling me away from the crowd watching the show, he practically pushes me with his cock until he has me where he wants me.

It's dark and the music is slow and hot. It's perfect music for fucking and teasing.

Moving to the front of me, he links an arm around my waist and pulls me against him. His body grinds against mine in a way that sends a shiver throughout my body. He definitely knows how to work his hips, and I have to admit that I'm extremely close to letting him just take me right here on the floor.

Spreading my legs with his knee, he places his leg between mine and grips the back of my neck, slightly dipping me backwards to whisper in my ear. "You know how much I love you riding my fucking face. It will be happening again tonight."

I grip onto the front of his shirt and move my hips with his when I feel one of his hands squeeze the bottom of my left ass cheek. Our bodies are as close as possible and I can feel the thickness of his erection poking me, driving me insanely mad.

The way he's moving against me is teasing the hell out of me and he knows it. This is his way of getting me back for the tease I just gave him in front of the whole room.

Grabbing my hand, he slides it in between our bodies and places it on his thick erection, moaning into my ear as I stroke it over the fabric.

Blaze looks extremely sexy tonight and *feels* even sexier. He knows this, but he also knows that we won't be fucking in a crowd. So this is just as painful for me as it is for him.

"This is your way of getting back at me?" I grip his dick harder, before playing with his head. "You started all of this in the pool the other night. You know you want to fuck just as badly as I do right now." I lean into his ear. "So let's see who caves first."

Smiling against his ear, I stroke him hard, while pressing my body into his. Knowing that it's too dark to see what's going on, I unzip his pants and slip my hand inside.

Breathing heavily as I wrap my hand around his bare cock, and squeeze, he slides his hand up the back of my dress and grips my ass. "Fuck . . . Karma. We can play this little game or I can take you into my office and fuck you like we both want." He slides a finger down the back of my dress and slides it up my ass crack. "I'm about to fuck this firm ass of yours."

I grab his hand and pull it away from my ass. "You're try-ing to go where no one has been before," I say, knowing it will only make him want me more. "Just imagine how bad your cock would hurt me then."

Smiling at the shocked look on his face, I walk away, know-ing that he'll be the one to cave in.

I've never even found the idea of anal play to be sexy before, but just the idea of Blaze inside of me, everywhere, has my body buzzing with excitement. I'll try anything with him. At least once.

I can hear Blaze following me up the private staircase. I don't even get half-way up, when I feel his face move up the back of my legs, then his teeth dig into my ass.

He bites me hard, while gripping my hips and stopping me from walking. "This ass is all mine, Karma. You have no idea what the fuck that does to me."

Removing his hands from my hips, I push down on his head and continue to walk up the stairs. Once I reach the top, he bur-ies his hands into my hair and presses me up against the wall.

I moan out as he presses his erection between my legs and grinds into me. "Stop running." He smiles against my lips. "I won't stop chasing. I think I've proven that by now."

My heart speeds up from the look in his eyes and I find my-self having to turn away.

What the hell is he doing to me?

"Look at me, Karma," he commands. "You want me. You can't hide behind that mask you put on. So just give in."

I shake my head, but on the inside, I know that he's right.

I've tried for weeks to keep my wall up around him and keep this all casual, but even lying to myself is becoming harder each day.

His heavy breathing only proves more that he's fighting

deep emotions for me.

I can't take it. This is all feeling too real to me all of a sudden. It's almost as if I can't breathe right now as I watch the way he's looking at me.

I see Blaze for who he really is in this moment and I'm scared. I'm truly scared of doing the one thing I promised I wouldn't do, fall for him.

"I need to go." I push him back to give me the space I need to breathe. "I can't do this emotion shit. I can't."

He grabs my arm and stops me, before I can walk away. "Don't walk out on me, Karma. It will only hurt us both. It's past the point of just being a quick fuck. And you know it."

"No," I lie. "It's not. Now let go, Blaze."

With force, he grabs my face and slams his lips against mine, kissing me deep and hard, taking my breath away.

I feel myself kissing him back, my heart racing faster than it ever has before. No one has ever made me feel the way I do when I'm with him.

Blaze is intense when he wants to be.

My hands grip at his hair, pulling as he picks me up and wraps my legs around his waist.

He doesn't hesitate, before he takes off down the hall, carrying me to his room as if the path behind us is on fire.

His lips don't leave mine as he kicks the door shut behind us and rips my dress off, just as he promised.

He's quick to undress himself and toss me back onto the bed, covering my body with his with a desperation that has me gripping at him as if my life depends on it.

He stops everything and stares at me. His eyes move over my face and it seems he's grasping for words to communicate what he wants to say and I watch in horror, trying not to feel crowded with anticipation and dread.

"I don't chase. Yet my ass seems to always be chasing you. Give me one fucking night where you don't run from my bed. Give me one night of you being real with me and give in to your true feelings and desires." He has me pinned beneath his body as he straddles my hips.

I swallow hard. He's too close and prying to be closer. "Blaze, please."

He watches me struggle with a response. He's ripped me of my clothing and is working on the wall that's surrounding my heart.

"I won't chase you again. I'm about to fuck you and how you react after this is on you. I've made myself clear on us. I want you. I haven't so much as looked at another woman to put in my bed since you were here the first time."

Tears form in my eyes and I fight to hold them back at the same time I'm frantically looking for words to say. I don't do all of this. It's complicated and I thought with a guy like him it would take a long time to be at this point. Yet, we seemed to have raced right to it.

He gets to me like no other man before him and that terrifies me.

"I can't." My two simple words seem to slap him in the face and I watch as he sits up to give me space, his eyes never leaving mine.

"You can. What's so bad about having a man crave you like I do? One that constantly wants to see you. Feel you. Fuck you. Get under that skin of yours and pull to the surface that spark you've buried so fuckin deep. Karma . . ." He leans back over me and begins to trail a path with his tongue over my chest. "Stop fucking fighting this."

I don't respond. I simply remain still and let him continue to speak to me through the movements of his body. He's different this time. His gentle touch and slow movements are complete opposite to any other time we've done this.

He begins kissing the crook of my neck and I work hard to get what he's just said out of my head. As always he feels good as he moves over me, but this time it's slow enough that I can anticipate his next brush of my skin. He's not being rough and fuck it if I find each breath even harder to take because I can feel him deeper than I've ever felt him before and he's not even thrusted inside me yet.

"Are you on the pill?" He interrupts my internal panic.

"Yes." I watch as something changes in his face. A hunger I'm used to seeing flashes over him and this is something I'm used to. Some sense of normalcy with what we have had in the past and it brings me slight comfort.

Before I know it, he has me flipped over and he's entering me from behind, pushing in deep and stopping. "Fuck, I've never been inside a woman this way. If this might be the last time we're together then I'm stripping us both bare. This is us. Nothing between us but what you have in your head."

I don't argue with him. In all honesty, I couldn't if I tried. My whole body is just craving the feel of him inside of me and I had no idea how bad I wanted him until he just sunk deep inside me. This is my first time not using a condom and honestly with how he feels around me, I don't want to right now.

We both know that I'm close to running. This might be our only chance to experience each other this way.

"Fuck, you're so warm."

"Blaze," I moan out as he pushes deeper and stops again. "I can feel all of you. Make it fucking count because this is my first time too."

Growling, he wraps one arm tightly around my neck and pulls me against his body, while moving inside me.

Everything about the way he's fucking me right now feels deeper than usual. Not just physically, but I'm trying to ignore all the rest.

I reach behind my head and wrap my arms around his neck, allowing his lips to capture mine as he leans around me.

We stay like this for what feels like forever, before he flips me over to my back and enters me slow and hard.

My nails dig into his back, my mouth seeking his as he keeps his slow torturous rhythm, never losing his momentum.

It's as if he has something to prove and he's not stopping until he does. "Your body is communicating what you can't seem to say."

"Stop talking about this. I just need to feel you." I close my eyes and slow the chaos inside, allowing my head to comprehend the unthinkable. Blaze has busted my wall down completely and I truly lie here vulnerable to his grasp on me.

He wraps his arms around me and lifts me onto his lap; we change positions a few times, never disconnecting.

I end up on top and he stops moving his hips. He's stripped us both bare and laid it all on the line while he waits for me to make a move.

Moving my hips slowly, my body betrays me as I do to him what I can't let myself say.

My emotions pull at my heart and it takes everything in me to move until he's panting and his hot release fills me and the warmth of it sends me over the edge myself.

I continue riding him until we're both completely down from our high. My hips finally stop grinding on him and now it's back to awkward. That was raw and now I sit here with his eyes staring at me as the chaos comes slamming back at me.

The urge for flight is overwhelming because the only alternative is to stay here and face what I refuse to admit.

Blaze has made his way through the barrier I use to protect me. Even though it's against everything I wanted to happen, part of me likes it.

Chapter

TWENTY TWO

Blaze

IT'S ALL IN KARMA'S HANDS now. I've spent the last couple of weeks chasing and showing interest in her that I've never shown in another woman and probably never will again. And to be honest, it surprises the shit even out of myself when I think about all of the times I went after her because she ran from my fucking arms.

We spent the whole night in my bed, her cuddled against my chest and my arms wrapped around her body. I kept pulling her close and couldn't shake the uneasy feeling that consumed me all night.

I could feel the need in her to run, but I could also feel her walls crumbling down around me. Her touch said everything she couldn't seem to say when I poured my emotions out to her.

Going back to the party was the last thing on my mind that night. I knew if I took Karma back downstairs that there was no fucking way I would've been able to get her in my bed again.

I needed to keep her there for as long as I could and continue to break her walls down and make her feel.

She's the toughest woman I've ever met and is extremely good at keeping people out. I have a feeling that her asshole ex is partially to blame for that or hell . . . maybe even fully.

It's been a few days since I woke up to an empty bed from her running from me again and I've yet to hear back from Karma. I sent her one text and that's all I plan to do until she has time to think and figure her feelings out. I won't push her until I have to, because you better believe that I will, before letting her go completely.

Security has been at her shop daily, just as they have with *Club Royal,* so that's the only reason that I haven't been outside her shop, making sure that she's safe from that asshole showing up again.

I look up at Luca when he splashes me. "Get that shit out of your head. You'll see her tonight for the show anyway. You can talk to her then."

Standing up, I yank my shirt off and toss it aside, before jumping into the water and swimming to the cooler full of beer.

"I'm good. Might as well spend the afternoon floating around the pool with someone who seems to be as lazy and just as handsome as my ass."

Luca laughs as I jump onto one of the mattresses and get comfortable with my beer.

"You're trying to tell my ass that you haven't been wondering who she's going to bring over to work on tonight on the live show?"

I shake my head and tilt back my beer. "There's no way Karma will be jumping to fuck anyone new anytime soon, brother. Now let's just relax and enjoy the fucking sun." I turn to him, while pulling my sunglasses down onto my face.

I really don't want anyone to see how shitty I'm feeling right now. "I'm going to need those jeans back, fucker. Make sure you wash them at least twice first. I don't know what the hell's gone on in them."

"And you'll never know, bro." He laughs and lies back, going quiet.

If anyone should understand that I need peace and quiet right now, it's my damn twin.

⁌⟋⟋⟍

THE LIVE SHOW STARTED TWENTY minutes ago and my heart is going crazy, knowing that Karma is set up just down the hall and within reach.

I saw the guy she walked in with and even though he kept checking her out on their way up the stairs, Karma kept her eyes on me, all the way up until they passed me to enter her new room.

I know I should stay out of her room and just let her do her job, so that's exactly why I canceled my call for the hour, and have decided to watch the live feed from my room.

The way he was looking at her didn't sit well with me, but I have a feeling that she locked her room so I won't get the opportunity to distract her.

She knows me well, because I would've been standing in the back of her room, reminding her of what she's missing out on and how much I want her.

I sit back in my chair and cross my arms, while watching Karma tattoo the top of the guy's leg.

Her left hand is close to his dick, holding up his boxer briefs and the closeness is enough to make my blood boil in anger and jealousy.

Her client is clearly hard and staring at her fucking cleavage as she concentrates on marking his skin. "Fucking bastard," I mutter to myself, while watching the comments roll in.

The computer is angled so you can see his leg and both of their faces, a little side table sitting close enough for the client to read the comments and respond if they wish to.

His eyes widen and he grins, while reading the comments. He's a good-looking guy and the thousands of women watching are only giving him more confidence.

Some of them are asking him to strip his shirt off, so he does, tossing it aside and flexing his chest for them.

Karma sneaks a peek, her eyes only checking him out for a few seconds, before she goes back to working.

Some women are telling him to either lose the boxer briefs or pull them up higher, so he pulls them higher up his tattooed legs and scoots down a little, making Karma's hand bump into his hard-on.

This only pisses me the fuck off and makes me want to break her door down, and show this asshole who she belongs to.

You can see the tiny smirk on his face as he watches her work on him. He says something too softly for the mic to pick up and then he reaches for her hand and places it on his dick.

I don't even wait to see Karma's reaction. My ass is down the hall and kicking her door in, before I have time to even breathe.

Karma looks up from telling her client off and gives me a look of shock, as I stand here breathing heavily, ready to kill this fucker if I have to.

"Blaze, don't," she begs. "I can take care of him myself."

She rushes over to me and places her hands on my chest, making sure that I don't get in the camera's view. "You kicking his ass on camera won't be good for either business. Don't," she says firmly.

Her client looks over at me and holds his hands up, showing

me that he's done. "Sorry, man."

"He touches you again and I'll rip his throat out. On live feed or not, I don't give a shit. His hands stay to themselves for the rest of this session or he loses them."

Removing Karma's hands from my chest, I pull up a stool and sit with my arms crossed, keeping my eyes on the asshole in the room for the rest of the hour.

He sits stiffly, barely even looking at the comments for the rest of the session.

After the camera cuts off, I get ready to throw the asshole out, but Karma grabs him by the balls and twists her hand, getting in his face, while she pulls him to his feet.

"Don't ever think you have the right to put my hands where the fuck you want them. I'm not like most women. Got it?"

He nods his head and holds his hands up in defeat, his face turning red, the tighter she squeezes.

I can't help but laugh at the fact that I'm actually witnessing this right now. I couldn't have imagined it any better than it went down. She handled herself in a way that will shut a man down at least for a second. The fact that she's not afraid to stand up for herself like that turns me the fuck on, but unfortunately that's not something I'll be acting on.

Hell, what doesn't turn me on when it comes to her? Fuck . . . this is the woman of my dreams.

"Now get the fuck out and don't come back to my shop again, Jameson."

He releases a breath at the same time that she releases his balls. "Shit . . . I meant nothing by it," he claims, out of breath. "I was only doing what the audience asked for. Didn't think it'd piss you off."

Luca appears in the door, looking confused as he looks the three of us over. He looks ready to throw down if necessary.

"Everything good in here?"

Karma gives Jameson a push toward the door. "Just go. I can't think right now."

"I'm sorry . . ." he starts.

"Just go," she says in frustration. "My second show and this shit happens."

My eyes stay on Jameson the whole way out the door. "Make sure he makes it to the door, brother."

"Damn . . . I'm gonna need to get filled in on this later." He takes off out the door, after the idiot that I'd like to strangle for touching her.

Being alone with Karma is tough; every part of my body aches to pull her into my arms, but I don't.

Maybe standing my ground with her will give her a reason to miss me. At least, I sure as hell hope so.

She turns to face me, her blue eyes burning into mine. I can tell that's she fighting her need for me just as badly as I am for her. Even her heavy breathing is giving her away.

"I'll have Rome come help you clean up. Next time, leave the door unlocked so we can get to you if we need to. Someone will be monitoring your show from now on to prevent this shit from happening."

I force myself to walk out the door, before my body gives into slamming her against the wall and fucking some damn sense into her.

Shit . . . I hope she figures this shit out fast. My dick can't take this rejection forever.

Chapter
TWENTY THREE

Karma

I WANT TO KICK HIS ass and then let him fuck me like his eyes already were. Damn him for making this complicated.

It takes me about thirty minutes to clean up my equipment and that is mainly because I've moved extremely slow thinking about Blaze. He doesn't get to make me crazy like this and then just act like it's an easy situation.

It's not. I'm not an easy person to be with and history has shown that. It broke me to walk out on him last time, but it's something I had to do. It's best for the both of us.

I can't do a relationship and that's obviously what he wants.

Rome steps through the door again and startles me when he speaks. "Do you need anything carried out? Or do you want to store it all here until next week?"

I've set up a complete station here to keep from having to haul it each week.

"I have a box to leave here if that's ok." I sound like a damn victim and that's pissing me off. Yes, this situation is weird, but there's no reason for me to feel like I do in this house. Coming in here tonight was weird and I almost called Lynx and cancelled.

If Charlie hadn't been in my ear to remind me of the cash flow, I would've probably worked something else out. In fact, that's something I can talk to Lynx about in the future. Sending out live feed from the shop may need to be something I need to start doing, simply just to stay out of all of the guys' way if nothing else.

This house is always busy and I'm sure if they really think about it, they'll see that it's better that way. If one of the guys want any work done, they can come see me there.

Rome leads me out the door and into the hallway that's full of memories for me. Blaze's room is next to Rome's and I'm hit with an unsettled rush of emotions when we pass by his door.

"Set it all there and I'll move it to one of the closets for you. Lynx said something about making one of our extra rooms yours soon, so it won't be long and you'll be able to just lock up and leave. This week we have a few guys coming in for interviews and he wanted to use the room you're in for that."

My eyes take in all the crazy furniture in his room and it's hard to even hear what he just said. I couldn't even tell you what half of this shit does, but I'd like to know.

He's talking, but I'm just looking in awe and it frustrates me that my first thought is that I wish Blaze had some of these for us to play on. "Did you need to see Blaze before you leave?" Rome's voice pulls me from my thoughts and reminds me that I need to get out of here if I truly want to make a point with him.

"No, I've got to get to the shop."

I'm not ready for a relationship. My life is too complicated and I've learned that men can't really handle my career. They start off thinking it's badass to have me as a girlfriend, then when my hours pull me from them and keep me out late, they begin to raise hell. Not to mention all the insinuations about my late nights that I've had to deal with in the past.

I refuse to explain myself and have to defend my actions every single day of my life. So it's best that I just keep it the way it is. I'm done with all of that.

Piercing and tattooing for a living isn't something everyone can handle, but it's my life and it's what I love doing. Even though Blaze seems to be the perfect person to understand a difficult career to accept, he's proven his over jealous ass can't really deal with all the hazards my job can have.

I make it down the stairs and almost out the door when Lynx walks in with Rebel, his girlfriend, stopping me as soon as they see me.

"How did tonight go?" Lynx questions with a sexy grin, while gripping Rebel's waist as if he can't get her close enough.

I dread telling him, but decide it's best if it comes from me.

"My client over stepped and Blaze kicked in the door and pretty much threatened to kill him. So yeah . . ."

Lynx's laughter startles me. That's the last thing I expected. He full on laughs for a few seconds before he replies.

"That fucking explains it." He looks at Rebel before she smiles and nods as if they both figured as much.

"Explains what?" I'm confused and this doesn't happen often.

"Why all the emails are asking for Blaze to be next week's session. They want to see the two of you interacting again."

I don't know how to respond to this news. Callers must've seen and heard more than I had hoped. Blaze is a favorite in the house and it's normal for them to want to see him, but I'm not sure that's something I can do.

"I'm already selling those calls," Lynx adds,

"People are pre-ordering the fuck out of them. I had Rebel

set you up for it because I remember Blaze volunteering for that. Here's your pay for tonight's show." He holds his hand out and laughs at the surprised look that has probably consumed my face right now.

I look down at all the zeros and any resistance I had planned to voice, has now been stopped by how much more money this check is than last week's.

Holy. Fucking. Shit.

"Wow. I expected this show to be slower since it wasn't one of your guys." I'm shocked at this check. Completely shocked. To make that in one night is insanity. Never in my wildest dreams, would I ever think I'd make this much in such a short time. I can hardly breathe right now while the numbers sink in.

"Last week built up the anticipation for this one and apparently you managed to do it again. Our reports do show that they want our guys in the room though, so we'll need to work something out with that. Other than that, don't doubt it . . . just be proud of it and embrace it. You're alphachat.com famous right now. Run with it."

The noise of a back door slamming forces me to say my goodbyes and get out of here before Blaze makes it all uncomfortable again.

Next week will be bad enough, but for that kind of money, I'll swallow my tongue and push my emotions back through the live feed. It should be easy hiding my feelings, it's what I'm great at.

I can hear voices around the pool, but it's the opposite way from where my car is, so I stay clear and walk fast, hoping I'm not noticed. I glance around the trucks and see that Blaze's truck is gone. I feel relief and an odd sadness falls all over me. He's doing exactly what I asked, by giving me space, so I don't know why that disappoints me.

My car is at the far end of all of the vehicles parked. And it's during my walk that I notice how clear the sky is. The stars are bright in the dark sky and for a second I just stop and take in the overwhelming beauty above me. Seems like it's been forever since I've had a moment to just stop and enjoy something so simple.

It only takes me a second to snap out of it when I hear a rumble of laughter coming from the pool again. I take off down the long driveway and get through the gates before I finally take a deep breath, trying to calm my insides.

I'm driving down the narrow road in deep thought when I notice a truck on the side of the road.

When I get closer, I see that it's Blaze's and I try to decide if I should stop or not. My instincts get the best of me and I drive by slowly, with the window down just to check on him.

He's laid out across the hood of his truck, his back against the windshield, and his hand in his pants. I notice his phone in his other hand just as I hear a female voice begin begging him for more.

"Pull it out, Blaze. Stroke it for me." He turns to look at me before he responds.

"Looks like you'll have to get me on the next call, Sweetheart. Our call ends in ten seconds."

"Thank you for taking me on a short date under the stars. It meant a lot."

His phone goes dark and he slides down the hood of his truck, instantly walking over to my open passenger window.

"You gonna beg me to pull it out too?"

My laugh could've been insulting if he wasn't purposely rubbing himself in front of me. He's always playful and so hard to stay away from.

That is until he gets all emotional on me.

"I was afraid you had broken down on the side of the road and stopped to see if you needed a ride."

"Oh I could use a ride, but you know that's every day." He never misses an opportunity to be dirty.

And fuck my life if I don't truly want to give him that ride.

He looks at me for a few seconds, before he opens my car door and reaches for my hand. "Sit with me for a few seconds. You looked stressed as fuck and I don't like that."

I breathe in his familiar scent as he leans over me to put my car into park. "I can't just leave my car sitting in the middle of the road."

"Yeah, you can. People will drive around."

I don't even get to resist him, because he pulls me out of the driver's seat and guides me over to the back of his truck, pulling the tailgate down.

He effortlessly picks me up and sets me down, before he jumps up beside me and places his hands behind his head for support as he lies back.

"Blaze . . ." I look back at him, hesitant on whether or not I should jump down and run now or see what he's trying to do. "What are we doing? I need some rest before I have to get back to the shop."

Blaze sits up and grips my shoulders, pushing me back, until he's leaning over me, his face close to mine. "We're taking a few minutes out of our crazy as shit lives and enjoying a moment together. I'm not asking for anything, but for you to just let your guard down for two minutes and relax."

My eyes meet his, just before he turns away and lies back down, looking up at the sky.

Releasing a breath, I lie back, joining him.

Even lost in the damn stars, all I can think about is crawling on top of Blaze's insanely sexy body and taking him for a ride.

I'd love for him to make me scream under the stars, but that isn't going to happen. .

I notice him look over at me every few minutes, but surprisingly, he doesn't make a move like I expected.

"It's so clear tonight and looks massive." My mind is finally calm and just taking in the moment. He doesn't respond, but slides his arm under my head and half way pulls me closer to him. It's almost a compromise to what I want, close but not too close.

We lie here in silence, enjoying the peace and quiet for what seems like twenty minutes or longer, before Blaze's phone goes off.

I sit up quickly, knowing that I need to take off, before I can even find out who's on the other end of that call.

"I need to go, Blaze."

He watches me as I jump down to my feet and walk over to get into my car. I'm just glad this isn't a heavily traveled road and my car wasn't in the way. Looking at how it truly is in the middle makes me feel guilty.

I take one last look back at Blaze before I put it in drive. He's holding his phone out, but doesn't seem in a hurry to answer it as I drive off, leaving him sitting there by himself.

Shit . . . why does that sight make my heart ache?

My mind isn't clear the entire drive back to my house. I try to sort out the chaos I'm feeling about Blaze, but the drive is too short to get anything accomplished.

Right now I can't get over the pull I have to go back to him, if only he'd keep things simple and easy.

I park in my driveway since I'll only be here a few seconds before I run to the shop. I need to load a few more things to take up there since my schedule was cleared for the Alpha House tonight.

It doesn't take me long to grab the things I need and before I get a chance to lock up, I see my ex, Ryan. My hands are full and I try to act normal when I see him even though he makes my insides erupt with hatred and regret.

The things this man has done to me in the past are most of the reason I can't let anyone near me today. His jealousy and insane logic were like a constant struggle and it got violent in the end. I knew I had to escape him before he managed to trap me further.

Opening this shop was my out. And I took it instantly, even though he just knew it would never work and there was no way I could survive without him.

I can now walk proudly knowing I've only just begun and my shop is already more successful than the trash hole he has.

"Ryan. What are you doing?" I keep walking to my car and he tries to stand in front of me along the way.

"I want to see you."

Crap. He's drunk. I can tell by his slur the second he opens his mouth.

"You've seen me. Now go." I try to make it seem like he isn't scaring me, but the reality of it is, when he drinks I can't predict what he'll do. This is when things get bad.

"No. I want to see you wrapped around my cock while I sink so deep into you that you'll remember where you belong."

He has no idea that he can't even reach that deep. There's not a depth inside me that believes I belong to this man.

"Your dick can't reach that far, Ryan. Go home." I manage to drop my things in the backseat of my car and close the door before he begins to move forward on me.

Walking fast, I hope to get back inside and grab the bag I take everywhere with me because it's where I have my gun. He's too fast and stops me just before I get inside.

His touch disgusts me and his eyes show just how bad he's fucked up. I can't believe that I let my guard down and I'm now stuck here with him with no protection.

My mind was focused on Blaze instead of everything around me.

He leans against me; luckily it's just his chest that I feel against me. There's not an erection bulging into my thigh as if this were Blaze. At least if it were Blaze, I'd know I was safe from the bad kind of pain.

Ryan runs his hand up my body and tries to cup my face. I'm not sure what fucked up thing he's trying to prove here, because the only thing he's proving is how right I was to stay away from him.

"This is mine and you're keeping it from me. I miss your face. Your lips. Your tits." His fingers touch each thing he says and the stench of his breath forces me to hold my breath as he does.

I hope this doesn't get worse than it has to. "Ryan, I told you to leave me alone. I'll call the police to get you hauled the fuck off."

He tightens his grip on my wrist and moves his mouth over mine.

"Not even the fucking police will keep you from me if I want to see you." His threat pulls me straight back into the past and I know this night is about to get bad.

I need him to leave and fuck my life, if I could just turn back time I never would've left Blaze's arms.

Chapter
TWENTY FOUR

Blaze

SITTING HERE WITH MY HANDS in my hair, I watch Karma's taillights as she takes off down the road, fucking running from me once again.

My phone buzzes from my lap, letting me know that I have a caller waiting, but the last thing on my mind right now is jerking off for someone other than Karma.

That's exactly why I ignored it the first time it went off in hopes that Karma would stick around.

"Shit," I say, once I realize what I'm about to do. I should leave her alone, but the thought of her out this late at night just won't let me.

I jump down and slam the tailgate of my truck closed, before jumping inside and taking off after her.

She's a few minutes ahead of me by now, but I head toward her house anyway, hoping that I'll catch her in enough time to at least make sure that she got inside safely.

My heartbeat pounds in my ears, my adrenaline pumping,

the moment I pull up behind her car to see her ex dickhead pinning her against the house, running one of his hands down her cheek.

When I jump out of my truck, she's pushing on his chest and yelling at him to leave her the fuck alone and move on.

She's so wrapped up in fighting him off that she doesn't even notice that I'm here yet.

I take off running through the grass, gripping him by the back of the neck and throwing him away from her.

Karma takes one look at my fear for her written all over my face and takes a step back, deciding not to try to stop me this time.

There's nothing in this world that could stop me from protecting this woman. Especially right here in this moment with this piece of shit trying to hurt her.

"Ryan . . . just leave." Karma watches me size her ex up as he struggles to get back to his feet, but keeps stumbling since he's so fucked up. "Go. Now."

I don't even give him the chance to stand completely up, before I jump down into the grass and place my foot on the back of his neck.

I bend down so he can hear me nice and fucking clear.

"Touch my woman again and I'll kill you if she doesn't first."

He laughs into the grass and attempts to push himself up with his hands, but I apply more pressure to the back of his neck, keeping him down.

"I'll always be near and watching. Just remember that," I repeat his earlier threat. "Don't think for one second that I won't."

"Fuck off and get off me. She's mine and she knows it."

Anger boils up inside of me from hearing him call her his. Fuck that. She'll never be his.

I scoot my foot up the back of his neck, to his head, smashing it down into the ground when he tries talking again.

"What was that, asshole?" I tease. "Couldn't hear you with a mouthful of dirt."

After a few seconds, I finally ease some of the pressure, giving him a chance to talk.

"Call your fucking watch dog off, babe. Karma . . . you know you're not done with me. You'll never be and we both know it."

I hear Karma grunt out in anger, before she jumps down next to me and pushes me out of the way so that she can get to him. "Fuck you, Ryan. Get up so I can make this as clear as possible."

Keeping my eye on his every move, I stand back and let Karma do what she has to do. He even attempts to touch her and I'll snap the fucker's neck.

As soon as he gets to his feet, Karma knees him in the balls and then in the face when he bends over to grab them in agony. She grabs his hair and yanks his head back for him to look at her, pulling hard. "Oh, we're done alright. Get that through your thick fucking skull or I'll let Blaze send you the message next time and he doesn't play quite as nicely."

She pushes his head back and then walks past me. "Get him out of my yard before I grab my gun."

Smiling from what I just witnessed her do, I wrap my arm around the asshole's neck from behind, and drag him up to his feet. If I wasn't so pissed right now, I'd be turned on as fuck by her. "You won't get anywhere near her again, so don't even fucking try. I'm not going anywhere and I'm not the only one that has her back."

Once we get over to his vehicle, I slam him against it and watch as he opens the door and crawls inside, before punching his steering wheel in defeat.

He punches it repeatedly, yelling something to himself, before taking off down that road as if he can't get away fast enough.

I immediately turn back around, my eyes landing on Karma. She looks so fucking hot, standing there with a determined look on her face.

When she doesn't speak, I walk toward her and pull her into my arms, wanting her to know how much I care about her. "Fuck, that scared the shit out of me. If he would've hurt you . . . are you okay?"

She wraps her arms around my neck, getting lost in me for a moment. Her heart is beating fast against my chest and her breathing is just now starting to slow down. "I'm fine. Just shaken up a bit."

I grab her face and press my lips against hers, catching her heavy breaths inside my mouth as I kiss her.

After a few seconds, she pulls away and turns her face out of reach. "Blaze . . . I need to go. I can't do this right now. I can't. I'm sorry."

"Karma . . ." I grab her arm as she goes to walk away. "Where are you going? I'll go with. I don't want you alone right now."

She shakes her head, backing up as if her feelings are too much for her to handle right now. I've never seen her look so damn scared. Something is hitting her deep right now. "I have to be at the shop. I'll be safe there so please . . . just not tonight. My head isn't clear. I don't even know what's up or down at the moment. I need to go . . ."

I release her arm and stand there like a fool, watching as she jumps into her car. She sits there for a few minutes, trying to hide her face from me, but I can tell that she's trying hard not to cry.

As much as I want to run over and comfort her, I know that you can only push Karma so much, before she runs. So I don't.

All I can do is make sure that she's safe as she takes off. My eyes watch her just to make sure that her driving seems okay, until she turns the corner and is out of sight.

I don't even know how long I stand in her yard, before I finally take off back to the Alpha House and close myself in my room and away from all the chaos of this place. I send a text to the security at K'inked before I truly feel relief knowing she's made it. I tell the guys to follow her home and let me know when they leave. Looks like I'll be sleeping in her driveway tonight if that's what it takes to make sure she's safe from that fucker.

I'm not even in my room for ten minutes, before Rome starts beating down my door, reminding me that we have a show in ten minutes.

"Better get your dick ready, fucker. Watch some damn porn if you have to. We're doing it in Levi's room."

"Fuck." I let out a breath and run my hands through my hair in frustration.

How the fuck am I going to pull this off when all I can think about is the look on Karma's face when she took off, leaving me standing there?

I lean my head against the wall and let the porn play in front of me, hoping like hell that it helps me get through this fucked up group jerk-off.

The tits on the screen do nothing for me because they're nothing like Karma's. The moans do nothing because they're fake as shit. Unlike Karma's.

"Fuck!"

Slamming my laptop closed, I let my thoughts wander to Karma and how sexy she looked the first night we fucked. The sound she made when I first sank into her is what does the trick for me.

By the time I get to Levi's room, Rome is standing in the

front, pulling his belt through the loop of his black jeans, teasing the person on the other end of the camera.

The woman's voice comes through telling him what to do next, before she asks Levi to step up and take his shirt off.

"Fuck, I can get through this," I try to convince myself as I close the door behind me.

As soon as I catch sight of Rome whipping his dick out, and stroking it, I shake my head and walk out of the room.

This shit isn't happening. Karma has me all fucked up . . .

I step into the hall and bump straight into my twin. "Thought you'd be busy for awhile, brother. What's got you running?" He catches the look on my face and nods instantly. "I got you. Go handle shit. They'd rather see my dick anyway."

I can't even laugh at his attempt to dig into me and catch a rise out of me. Normally it would work, but tonight I'm too worked up to even think clearly.

"Thanks. Just don't fuck it up." I keep walking and slam the door to my room once more. I hit the remote to my stereo and blast the music, no doubt letting it be heard outside of these walls. I don't have any fucks to give and just need a damn minute to decide what the fuck I'm going to do to get through to Karma.

She needs to be reminded of our chemistry together and apparently I need to show her that I won't be like any of her past dicks. Maybe that's what's keeping her distant. After the shit I've seen her ex do in just the short time I've known her, I could see why she's not rushing into anything.

I impatiently wait for the call that she's leaving the shop and before I'm in my truck, I get the text saying she's safe at home. The security guy I hired follows her home and then waits for me to pull up next to him before he takes off.

I pull my truck behind her car and turn off the engine, before walking around her house just to check things out. Everything looks in place and it seems like that fucker has decided to stay clear for now anyway.

Her house is dark with the exception of her bedroom window. The curtains are closed and I can't see anything, but I know she's in there when the light goes off.

My mind flashes with memories of us against her bedroom window as I walk back to my truck. The night air is sticky, but it's not going to bother me sleeping out here with my windows down. I can hear everything and will know if he tries to come back. My truck should keep him clear anyway.

I don't have my seat reclined before the front door flies open and Karma walks out in a robe.

What the fuck is she thinking?

That is a fuck me robe and that face of hers, along with her sassy ass walk, show she's pissed off and to me that's hot as hell and means it's time to fuck out some frustrations.

But I'm guessing that's not what she's stomping out here for.

"What in the hell are you doing out here? Blaze, what do you not understand about me needing some fucking space?" Her temper makes me smile and she doesn't slow down until she's opened the driver's side door. "Why are you here?"

I slide my legs out and let my feet hit the driveway before I grab her and turn us both and lean into her with her back against the side of my truck. "This is me giving you space. Do you feel my dick inside of you? No. That's space, Karma."

"Coming here late at night is not giving me space." Her breath hits my face as she stands strong with her response.

"That fucker will not touch you and if it takes me sleeping in your fucking driveway, then so fucking be it. Don't try to stop me." I speak right into her face, our eyes glaring into each other and our hearts both beating with adrenaline and a temper that only matches each other's.

"Don't be ridiculous. I don't need you to protect me." She shoves against my chest and I step back enough to let her move out from in front of me.

"Didn't say you did." I turn slowly and watch her pace with frustration a few feet before she turns around to walk back toward me.

"I know what you're doing. You're making me crazy. Stop rescuing me. Stop making it so that I'll run into you. Stop looking at me like that. And stop smiling at me when I yell at you."

"I do what I want. Haven't you figured this out yet?" She throws her arms up, irritated and I can literally feel my dick twitching as I watch her act with so much emotion. This tells me I get to her; whether she likes to admit it or not, I do.

"No. I do what I want. And right now you're trespassing."

"Call the police then. I'm not leaving here willingly until I know you have the security you need from that fucker." She paces a few more times before she finally starts walking back to the door.

"Fine then. Have fun out here if you have nothing better to do."

The sound of the door slamming has me shaking my head at her. I'm about done with this shit. In fact, tomorrow night will be when I give her no other option but to face what we have and how she needs to just let me in.

Because whether she likes it or not, I'm already there. Deep inside her in so many ways that she can't shake me even if she's tries.

Chapter
TWENTY FIVE

Karma

HE MAKES ME FURIOUS. HOW can he think this is normal and acceptable? I'm so damn frustrated and it's pissing me off that the more I walk away from him, the more I notice how hard it is to be near him. When I'm close to him, my body craves him so much more now. If he would just keep his space, I wouldn't have all these roller coaster emotions to deal with.

Tonight he's here and I can feel him all around me. The draw my body has toward his is driving me mad. I'm not supposed to feel again and damn it, he's forcing me to deal with him as often as he can.

I look out the window once more before I give in and put my clothes back on.

Damn you, Blaze . . .

He can't stay out there all night. There's no way I can handle him in my driveway. He's so close to me and I need him to go away for good. He knows that and doesn't care what I think or want and that makes me so irate.

He acts like he's giving me space, but everywhere I turn he's there. If he's not at the shop, he's on my damn mind in some way or another. So that is not giving me space. Maybe I need to just talk to him and tell him all the reasons why what he wants are impossible. I don't see any other option at the moment.

I pull up my hair and attempt to look as unattractive as possible before I open the door again and step outside. This time he's on the hood of his truck again, watching me as I approach.

"Did you get your gun to run me off?" He doesn't even sit up or look concerned. He freaking knows I could never hurt him and his confidence only proves this is going to be much harder than I want it to be.

"We need to talk."

He shifts his legs together and hits the hood slightly with his hand, never letting the other one free from behind his resting head.

"Bout fuckin' time."

The streetlight catches his face just right for me to see his expression. He watches me with those insanely sexy eyes that always seem to shoot right through me and break me down. I climb onto the hood and take a seat beside him, making sure not to touch him along the way. His eyes are heavy on me and damn it, I can picture them even in mostly darkness.

"We need to talk, but stop looking at me like that, Blaze. I can't be serious when you look like that."

He lifts a brow and then changes his facial expression so fast and serious, that I have to fight back the laughter at the odd look on his face. "Is this face unsexy enough for you? Or should I just cover it so you can concentrate?"

Smiling, I slap his shoulder and get comfortable, crossing my legs. "You're such a cocky pain in the ass . . . I don't know what to do with you half the time."

"You've done great things with me so far, babe. Lots of fucking great things. Now talk to me. I'll be here all night."

He positions his body so that he's facing me. His face still in that awkward ass position just to mess with me.

"I'm no good in a relationship, Blaze. Every single one that I've ever been in has ended in shit. Guys can't handle what I do and I have no urge to fight and prove myself every day to a man. I'm faithful and worthy of their love and devotion and I shouldn't have to verify that every night when I walk through the doors."

Blaze opens his mouth to interrupt me, but I quickly cover his mouth, causing him to bite my hand.

"Let me continue before you say anything. There's so much more I need to get off my chest. Got it?"

He kisses the spot on my hand that he just bit and nods his head for me to continue.

"Ryan was no exception to this. It started out with him being suspicious of my late night session, asking me questions and interrogating me until the point that he almost made *me* believe that I was lying. It even got to where he'd follow me when he got the chance and even go after some of my clients when he'd see them leave the shop."

"I couldn't handle it anymore. I was stressed and depressed to the point that I'd given up on fighting his assumptions. I just let him believe what he wanted because I knew nothing I said was going to make him believe any differently. I quit fighting him about it and he took it further. Thought he could beat the shit out of me to punish me for his insane dreamt up bullshit." I watch him clench his fist next to his leg, but cho0se to continue. He has to hear why this is all hard for me.

"He wanted to control me then. He tried both mentally and physically. I knew I had to get the fuck away and start my own shop and a new life. I wanted to escape any part of my life where that had been me. That weak little bitch who just tried to stay quiet and hope shit would pass."

Blaze sits up straight, his jaw clenching in anger. "Where the fuck does he live?"

I reach out and grab his arm, when I think he's about to jump down to the ground. His fist is still clenched tight, but he opens it up for me when I slide my fingers over it. "Blaze, no. I don't need you hunting him down and killing him. The last thing I want is you behind bars for me. No," I grind out. "If you want me to talk, then sit there and don't move. Just listen. I need you to listen."

I can tell that he wants nothing more than to take off right now and find Ryan, but he sits back, his muscles flexing as he waits for me to continue. "It's important that I stay strong and independent as a woman and I see you breaking me down and I just don't know how to take it. I swore off any relationship and when I went to the Alpha House that first night, the last thing I expected was for you to want more than what it has to be." He's fidgeting and I can see him struggle to stay quiet. I have to continue and make sure he knows how I feel since I haven't been able to say it in the past.

"I love spending time with you, but beyond that I can't promise you or even give you hope of anything more."

"Well damn. Here I was about to ask you to marry me and move in to the Alpha House. My laundry needs to be done and dishes should be kept clean." He lies back against the windshield again, his head resting on his arms behind him.

"You're not taking me seriously. I'm just wasting both of our time." Before I can move more than an inch, his hand closes down on my wrist, stopping me.

"I'm hearing you, and I'm just going to wait until you're ready to hear me." He keeps his grip for a few seconds before brushing his fingers up the inside of my arm as he pulls away.

What can he possibly say that he hasn't already? It's the weight of all of it that's been heavy on me for awhile now. I guess this is the best time to get it all out. I decide to let him say everything he needs to because it's best if we leave it all out on the hood of his truck.

"Alright, I'm listening." I give in and let him say what he needs to.

"The fact that you're a strong independent woman is the reason I'm so attracted to you. My goal is not to control you, but to encourage you to live life, constantly safe and happy. If I make you scream anything, it'll be my name as you come over and over while I'm doing nothing but pleasing you in that bed . . . Or wherever we decide we can't keep our hands off each other." I swallow hard as he continues to talk, saying all the perfect things to make this even harder to take in.

"You won't ever get questions from me and I'm guessing you understand that I know how a career could be hard for someone to handle. It's something I've thought long and hard about, because I don't want to stop working at the Alpha House. I'm just getting started and have so many ideas for growth. One of them making your show more successful each week." The more he talks, the louder I hear what he's saying.

"I have no intention of changing your path in life, only hoping to get to walk beside you and all that mushy shit." I laugh at his way of getting rid of some of the heaviness of this conversation.

"Nice. Mushy shit, huh?"

"I'm not about to get deep in all that when I know that'll make you slide that fine ass off this truck and run again. I get it. I make you feel and you didn't want to feel me. Well, guess what . . . I'm real big for you not to feel." He grabs himself and laughs in a playful manner, making me smile at his teasing. He just seems to always amuse me with his humor and it makes for a more relaxed time when I'm with him like this.

"Can you ever be serious or is it always about your cock with you?" I lie back on the windshield and look at the sky while I wait for his response. He's careful not to reach for me or hold me and I honestly notice it immediately.

"Well, it's definitely an important part of my day, but it also keeps you smiling when I taunt you. What can I say, I'm used to using it as a tease so it's just where I start."

"Were you really going to sleep out here?"

"Yep. Sure as hell was. I don't want him getting anywhere near you." My heart actually skips a beat with his response. I hate how I came at him when all he was doing was trying to protect me. It makes me feel like a giant bitch.

"Sorry I yelled at you. Thank you for trying to watch over me, but you know you can't sleep out here." I can't expect him to do something like this.

"It's about time you let me back in your bed. I've been waiting on you to come to your senses." He sits up and slides off the truck. His grip on my ankles is the next thing I feel before he drags my ass across the hood until I'm being lowered to stand on my feet.

"That's not what I meant and you know it." He smiles back at me, confirming he knew what I was meaning.

"I know, but you can't blame a guy for trying." He stops talking and just looks at me. I wait for him to say something to tease me, but he doesn't.

"Stop thinking so much. Just let it all happen as it does. I won't pressure you into anything more than just knowing you're protected. I'm not leaving here tonight, so just go inside and get your rest. Let me watch over your house and we can both feel safe." He's out of his mind if he thinks I could ever let him sleep on top of his truck. Hell, I'm practically rubbing my legs together to keep from climbing him again and letting him do what we both want.

"Just come inside, but don't get any damn ideas from this. Being fuck friends is still all I can handle."

"That I can deal with." He moves to lock up his truck and I feel relief that all of that is over. I've told him what I can handle and he seems to understand that's all I can give.

It's up to him now to keep his end of the bargain and let me be me and I'll let him do his thing.

I just need to remember that doesn't mean we can't both meet up and do each other when we feel the need.

Chapter TWENTY SIX

Blaze

SHE'S MAKING IT HARD TO not grab her and carry her inside. I fight the urge like I've never had to. Talking to her only made me want her more.

I understand where she's coming from, but that doesn't mean I have to give up on what I really want. It seems like she's a little more relaxed and maybe I can lay off a little and she'll come around, but with me that isn't really likely no matter how much I tell myself that's the plan.

I'm obviously making it too easy for her to push me away, maybe it's time she knows what it feels like to have someone fuck and run. First I'd have to pry myself away from her and I don't see that happening either.

"Just come inside, but don't get any damn ideas from this." The hunger in her voice is music to my ears. *I won't get any ideas that aren't already there, that's all I can promise.*

"That I can deal with." I'll have to take what I can get with her until she comes around. Something tells me my plan to make a little change in my game will have her rethinking her rules.

I quickly lock up my truck and follow her inside. Even with her hair pulled up and these hideous shorts she's wearing, I'm still looking at her like I always do. She can't even hide behind all of that ridiculousness with that body of hers.

She's silent all the way through her house and up the stairs to her bedroom. I'm slow to move inside her room, allowing her to make the first move. Is she wanting me to sleep next to her, or are we doing this my way?

She slowly unbuttons her shirt and slides her shorts down her legs. I watch her naked body while she pulls the elastic out of her hair, shaking it out as it falls around her shoulders.

Her nipples are hard and her skin is flushed, but it's her eyes that I'm drawn to. She's craving my touch and it might just be time to make her beg a little.

I don't move a muscle while I watch her slide her fingers between her legs and taunt me. She squeezes her thighs together and makes a few noises to tempt my resistance, but I hold strong.

It's not until she opens her mouth that I rub my hand over my erection. "You like to watch, don't you?" *Fuck yes I like to watch. Give me a fucking show that I'll never forget.*

"I do." *Keep it simple.*

"I'm new at this, so don't judge too harshly." She slips the same two fingers in her mouth and sucks them in until her cheeks hollow.

"Quit wasting your time on your fingers. I'll give you something to suck on." She smiles at me as she slides them out of her mouth and over her nipples.

"I figured you'd say something like that. Maybe I like the way I taste." Holy fuck. She needs to stop talking before I fuck the words right out of her damn mouth. *Stay back. Make her come to you.*

"You can still taste yourself on my cock. Give me five minutes and you'll really get to savor greatness." Her eyes open slightly as she takes in my bold response. I can do this all day. Hell, I practically do already, but this is the first time I've truly wanted to make all of my threats and promises a reality.

She slips her fingers in deeper, pressing her tits together as she does.

"You like it when I talk dirty, look at you clenching your thighs together wishing it was my big dick inside you. Instead you're stuck with those pretty little fingers of yours."

"Stop playing around and fuck me."

"You do realize this means nothing and I can't do anything more with you than this right here." I tease her further, repeating her own words back at her as I kick off my jeans. "Good thing it's what I do best. Get on your knees, I think it's time your mouth is properly introduced to my dick."

She goes to her knees as I approach her with my hard on in my hand. Her grip around the base has me releasing it while I stand there and take in the feeling of her tongue swirling around.

I can't resist guiding her even deeper when she takes it to her throat and holds me there. With my grip on her head, I fuck her mouth until she's literally gagging and drool is running down her chin. She doesn't get up and even goes back for more.

"Get on the bed. I want that pussy." She does exactly as I say and even looks better than I imagined. Her ass is fucking unreal and I can see how wet she is from here while she positions herself on all fours at the edge of the bed.

"You can almost feel me inside you, can't you? Your tight grip as I slide in and out of you until you can't stand it any longer."

"Yesss. That's what I want. Just stop talking and get over here." I slide on the condom like the pro I am and drop everything else on the floor.

I do as she begs and make it a point to enter her just like she wants. Hard and fast. She doesn't get any more foreplay. We've had enough of the back and forth teasing and it's time to fucking get to the good stuff.

"So good," she whimpers through her words and I keep up a steady rhythm. It's my pleasure to make her forget all the bullshit she's been stirring in that head of hers. She's mine and she'll soon realize that herself. Until then, I'll just remind her every chance I get.

"Fuck yes." I can't hold back the fast pace and I literally fuck her over the edge of her release and straight up to my own before I purposely slow down to make it all last longer.

I lean over her and slide my hands over her body, appreciating every single inch of her.

"Turn over. I want to watch you." We move positions and something clicks in me as I watch her watching me. She's trying to hide what she's feeling, but I can see right through her. She feels me. She feels us. And it's my job to make sure she never forgets what she's feeling right now.

I slide in slow and never let my eyes fall from hers. She's searching my face and chest as I move over her with each thrust until she leans her head back and closes her eyes. It's all too much for her to take, so I slow down even more and make her look at me again.

"*Watch me*, Karma," I whisper against her neck and she instantly opens her eyes. She slowly slides her fingernails across my back and I know she's just trying to encourage me to lose it like normal, but I'm not going to. She's always taken me fucking her, but this time I'm going to show her how I can also make love.

This will be a first for me. I don't do this, but I seem to say that a lot when it comes to Karma.

Her eyes shift again and I move in and out of her slowly,

making sure to feel each breath of hers against my face.

This is real. She can try to run from what we have, but when it comes down to it, she can't stay away.

We move as one for hours until we both release together. I pull her against my chest and hold her afterward, staying awake the rest of the night. Listening to her every breath made me think all night.

I want this woman in my life. I want to see her everyday, fuck her every day. Hell, I want her in my bed and in my way all damn day.

She's not there and it sucks to be this into someone who won't allow you in, even though you know you belong there.

I slide out of bed and quietly pull my clothes on when I first see the sunlight coming through the window. She wants that space, I'll give it to her. It might do her good to wake up and find that I left her for once.

If this doesn't work, I'll just fucking grab her and tie her to my bed until I can convince her what we have is real.

Chapter

TWENTY SEVEN

Karma

I WAKE UP TO AN empty bed and a hollow feeling in my chest, at the fact that Blaze slipped away and left me in the middle of the night.

My mind instantly replays the events of last night and the more I think about how it felt when he made love to me and then held me close, the more the emptiness in my chest grows. I can't shake this aching feeling I have for him.

He's made me feel things I never thought I'd feel. His words, his lips and his body awakened something in me, making me realize that I'm in too deep with him to crawl my way out and just pretend that I don't want him for more than just sex.

This feeling . . . in my chest. The ache . . . it's real. There's no denying it. It confirms everything I've been trying so hard to deny. I can't walk away from this man and in fact, I want nothing more than to go to him.

Closing my eyes, I inhale and then slowly exhale, while trying to figure out how I'm going to get through this day before the live show tonight. He's consuming my mind and I still need to function outside of the world of Blaze.

Lynx set up a meeting with a couple of his artist friends at my shop and I'm supposed to be there in less than an hour to check out their portfolios.

How the hell am I supposed to even concentrate with the flood of emotions washing through me right now?

"Damn you, Blaze. You always find a way to get to me . . ."

I find myself in a daze, doing my morning routine without much thought, before I'm pulling up outside my shop. It doesn't matter how I feel right now. This has to be done this morning. My shop is the most important thing to me and getting more artists in here is a must. The calls since we started the live shows have become insane. We're working on one hell of a call back list to contact once my new guys get started.

That should be a great incentive for them to come to work for me, not many can walk in to a full client schedule like I'm about to hand over to them.

My mind shifts back to Blaze again. Why can't I get him out of my mind? It shouldn't be this hard to focus. "Get a damn grip, Karma." I talk out loud as I look at myself in the mirror.

All of my thoughts of Blaze will have to wait until tonight. I can't deal with all these emotions and confusion while I'm in the shop; Charlie will call me out on that shit right away.

When I step out of my car, Charlie is leaning against the side of the building, talking and laughing with one of the guys Lynx must've sent for the shop.

He's tall, in shape and inked up from head to toe. Exactly how Charlie likes them. Let's just hope that his artwork looks as good as he does for her sake.

Charlie and the tatted up hottie look my way and smile. I walk over and stop in front of them before I reach out and attempt to shake his hand.

The guy smiles and tosses his cigarette down, before holding his hand out to take mine. "You must be Karma, I'm Gage, and I hope like hell that you like my work because this shop is where I plan to be."

I smile and grab his hand, giving it a quick shake, before turning to Charlie to see her beaming.

"I hope so too, Gage." I need something to go right today. "Let's step inside and I'll take a look."

He nods his head and pulls a folder out from under his arm. He guides Charlie to go in front of him and I see him checking her out as I unlock the door and let us all in.

"I'll be over here," Charlie says happily. "I'll gather the paperwork."

I laugh and watch Charlie looking through the drawers for the paperwork we give to new all new contract artists to fill out. "What makes you so sure that we'll need those papers?"

"Because I already looked at his work. Fucking beautiful! My eyes could hardly handle it and he's doing my next piece."

Gage lifts a brow and smiles at me with a confidence that I like. I could definitely see him fitting in well with the rest of the shop.

I shake my head at Charlie and let her go about her business, while Gage begins pulling out his portfolio shots and displaying them on the glass countertop.

My eyes widen with each drawing he pulls out; he is damn talented and has a perfect dark twist to his designs that intrigue the hell out of me. I even find myself gasping at one. *Hell, he may be doing my next piece.*

My heart is racing with excitement and relief that I've found someone that will fit perfectly. I almost have an urge to scream that he's hired before he changes his damn mind.

"Wow . . ." I find myself touching his work, tracing my

fingers over it. "Your work is brilliant. It's not very often that you see someone with such talent. I want you in my shop. Let's talk details if you're interested."

Gage smiles and runs a hand through his long, dark hair, slicking it back. "That's the answer I was hoping to get. Lynx has told me a lot about your business and I'd love to be a part of it."

"Great." I turn to Charlie and smile. "Today's your lucky day, sweets. Get him in the system and set up. I'm gonna mess around with a few things in my room before the second guy shows up."

Charlie doesn't even look at me when I speak to her. She's too busy ogling over Gage.

Having her distracted only gives me more space to sit back and try to get my thoughts of Blaze in check.

I find myself checking my cell for any text messages or missed calls from him, but nothing. Not a word from him since he left my bed. This disappoints me much more than I would've ever thought.

My mind stays on Blaze, until Charlie pushes my door open and pokes her head inside. "Myles is here. I already have him pulling out his artwork for you."

"Thanks," I say softly, keeping my eyes on my phone.

I hear the door close and think that she's gone, until she speaks again. "Are you okay? You seem a little out of it today."

I nod my head and set my phone down. "I'm fine. Just thinking about things that I shouldn't be." I stand up and offer her a small smile. "So does Gage still have your attention or is this *Myles* guy your new distraction and target?"

She laughs and opens the door. "I guess you'll see for yourself. You know I don't like to limit myself to just one guy to flirt with. There's plenty of Charlie loving to go around."

I follow her out the door and am happy to see Gage and Myles talking and showing each other some of their work. I can tell from the expression on Gage's face that he's impressed with Myles' work, which is my first clue that he'll be our second new guy for the shop.

And from the look of these guys, I won't be surprised if they bring in a whole new set of clients, lining up to get tattooed from the hot new guys. Should've known anyone that Lynx knows is ridiculously good looking and will be perfect *eye candy* for the damn shop. It won't hurt the shop one bit to have these guys in house.

I'll have to be sure to thank Lynx later for sending his guys my way. Just another thing that'll keep the business flowing and the shop growing. It's their talent that matters to me, but their good looks are just a damn bonus that will draw more women in.

The sound of the door pulls my attention from the guys and I turn to see a sexy female make her way to the front counter. I eavesdrop and hear Charlie ask her what she can do for her and hear Lynx's name yet again so I make my way to introduce myself.

"Hi, I'm Karma and this is my shop, how can I help you?" She looks a little nervous, but quickly shakes it off when she shakes my hand.

"My name is Envy and Lynx told me you're looking for some help here." He really came through for me and it couldn't be happening soon enough.

"I need help desperately. What can you do?" I lean against the counter and watch her respond to me. She's young, but I can tell she's artistic by the way she's dressed and all the work she's showing off on her own canvas.

"I have experience with piercing and thought maybe I'd see if I could do some time here and work towards what I really want to do, which is tattooing. I work for him at Club Royal, but he told me he'd work something out with you if you're interested in letting me work here." I smile instantly. We could use another girl in the house to even things out a bit, even if she's fresh meat. If she took most of the piercings off my schedule, then I can handle the tattoos and things will definitely speed up for the shop.

"When can you start?"

"I can start tonight. Lynx thought you might want me to sit in on the live feed to help with the Q&A part of the show." Her cool composure is an instant draw to me and if I'm this quickly attracted to her personality, the live viewers will respond well to her. I see what Lynx is doing here and I have to say I appreciate the hell out of it.

"Can you be there by seven?" She smiles instantly and I feel great knowing I'm about to get some relief in here.

"Lynx told me Blaze suggested I talk to you to start with. I'm so glad he thought of me." There it is. Blaze floods my mind again. This time I can't be frustrated because I needed this. And now I feel like I need to see him even more than I did when I walked through these doors.

There are so many great things about this moment that should have me wanting to celebrate.

But all I can think about is Blaze. I need this day to hurry the hell up . . .

Chapter
TWENTY EIGHT

Blaze

WALKING AWAY FROM HER SUCKED completely. But knowing she'll be here tonight is making me less irritable and helping me keep my shit in check.

"Jesus, you look like shit. Did you pull an all nighter or something?" Luca walks in while I'm pouring my sixth cup of coffee for the day.

"Yeah, you could say that."

"Everything alright? You know I can kick someone's ass if I need to." He grabs the coffee pot and pours his own cup before he saunters to the other side of the bar.

"I may hold you to that. There's a fucker I need to visit today. Wouldn't hurt having someone else there to drive my point home."

His eyes meet mine and everything that's ever come between us disappears into the depths of nothing and I know right away that he's in for anything I need. It's how brothers are. I know he's not the only one in this house that would do the same, so I decide to really make a fucking point.

"How about in an hour, we take a road trip? I'll get the guys together and we can parade our asses to his fucking shop in a convoy he'll never forget. There's an asshole I have an appointment with today."

He nods and takes a big drink of his coffee before he responds.

"Let me get my hair pulled back and my mean face on. I'll be ready for anything." He walks out of the room and I hear Rome outside talking by the pool.

I may as well drive my logic straight through that mother fucker's head and take all the guys. He needs to know that if he even calls Karma, I'll be so far up his ass, he'll feel me yanking out his insides before I even get near him.

"Hey Rome. I need all of you guys to help me make a run. Need to let a guy know I mean business and I may as well show him what he's up against right away."

He looks over at me from his phone call and hangs up quickly.

"I'm in, brother. When?"

"An hour. Can you get all the other guys around? Luca already knows, but I need the rest. I need to call Lynx about a few things before I lose track of this entire fucking day."

"You got it." I slip inside and make my way to the office. Lynx and I have been working on security at every location, including Karma's shop. We've also been looking at people to bring in to the house for different jobs and I had to push him to get some artists in to help her. I just hope it will relieve some of her stress and let her enjoy life for a fucking minute.

"Hey, Lynx. You're always right on time, aren't you?" I hit the speaker button and lean back in the chair.

"You can't run a business like this being late all the fucking time. Learn something from me and who knows what you'll be able to do."

"I'm here too, fucker. Right on time. What's on the agenda?" This is how we talk to each other. It's a mutual pain in the ass respect that we have going and honestly, I owe him so much for giving me an opportunity to work for him. This company has made a huge change in my life and I can't even imagine doing a desk job somewhere answering to some snooty fucking dick every day.

"I sent those guys you suggested to K'Inked. Hopefully she'll take them in. I have one in mind as well and I figure he'll be in town next week. Also, Envy was excited when I gave her the go ahead. Let's talk about another Alpha for the house. Have you had time to look at the guys I sent you?"

I sit up and start thumbing through the names he sent over. I looked at them all but none of them stood out.

"What if we changed it up a bit? How about I bring a girl into the house and we can tap into the men of the world? Who knows, we may end up with an entire house of women just to meet demands if it all goes well."

He's silent for a few minutes and I know he knows it's a great idea.

"I like the idea, I'm just worried about dropping a female in a house full of Alphas. It can only be a disaster waiting to happen."

"I'll lay down the law before she comes in," I assure him. "They won't choose pussy over money and they'll know I'll boot any of them who fuck up. You know it's an entire audience we aren't even reaching and this is our in."

"You're right," he responds after a few seconds. Can we set it up on a probationary period of thirty days and see what the numbers do and how the guys handle a female in the house?"

"That was my plan."

"Look at you running this place without me. Maybe I need to think about being more silent and let you do this for awhile. I've been dying to take Rebel on a long trip and it may just be about time."

"Let me know when you leave. I've got this place."

"I heard you've been spending extra time with Karma . . . Anything you want to admit?" He's fishing and for once I'm not going to try to deflect his questions about a female in my life.

"I'd spend even more time if she'd stop thinking so much. But for now, we're just having fun."

"I remember that shit all too well. Someone told me some important advice once. If she doesn't come to you, take your ass to her and give her no choice."

I have to smile as he gives my own words back to me. That's my plan, I'm just trying to let her get to the point where she'd actually be ready for me and what I want.

"I'll have to work on that."

He's laughing before I can finish my sentence.

"You're the last one I thought would get all caught up. You sure you can stay in the house after all of this?"

"I have no plans of leaving the house, so just count me in on any business that you need handled."

"If anything, you can always slow your call load a little and I'd love to seriously talk to you about taking an official position as house Alpha. Of course, I'd compensate you for all the shit you'll handle that I won't have to deal with. Think on it and we'll talk about it next time."

"Don't need to. I'm in." I don't hesitate to jump on this opportunity. It'll only allow me to do what I've been enjoying, looking for business opportunities to expand this company.

"Alright. I'll talk numbers with you next time and consider

yourself hired for the job. Just don't let me down and I won't have to put my foot in your ass."

"You couldn't catch my ass."

He laughs even louder before he says his goodbyes and hangs up on me.

That call went even better than I hoped and now I know the changes I'm about to make are going to only make this house better. He knows my ideas are phenomenal and have all worked. He's always asked my opinion on things so this new job for me seems to be the perfect set up.

I spend some more time looking at the pictures in front of me, focusing on the girls I had in mind. A few of the girls from Club Royal are in here and even a few from my hometown.

The door opens and I watch Levi strut in and start talking. "Looks like I'm about to get in on some ass beatin' action. Tell me who we're fuckin' up today!" He's entirely too excited for this, but I have to say it makes me feel good to know he has my back like this.

"Karma's ex dickhead. He thinks he can rough up a woman, so he needs to be taught a lesson he won't forget."

"It'll be my pleasure to hand him his ass. Oh . . . damn. What are you looking at here?" He points to a few of the girls on my desk.

"I'm looking to bring a female into the house."

He doesn't let me continue before he's lifting a few of the pictures from the desk. "Holy fuck. Get Envy in here. I'd pay to see her. Hot damn, that woman does it for me." His excitement makes me laugh and I rip her pictures from out of his hand.

"I'll be making that decision and just so you know, it would make her off limits. House rules are about to change."

"Yeah, yeah. She deserves the kind of money this place can bring in though. I'd keep my distance to give her a chance like this. She's a damn fine woman and runs that club like a fuckin' pro."

"We need to get on the road if we're going to get this done before we have to be back tonight. Will you see if the rest of the guys are ready?"

"Sure will, boss." I toss the pictures down and look at my phone. I was hoping for a text from Karma, but no such luck. Guess I'll just have to wait until tonight to see her. "Let's fuckin' do this!" I step out onto the balcony and see them all ready and waiting for me in the main foyer. They've all put on the roughest clothes they own and they make me laugh at their ridiculous energy. "Well I wanted to scare him to death, not fuckin' make him die laughing. Can we please work on our delivery here? How about you just follow my lead."

Nash and Knox both shake my hand when I get to the bottom of the stairs. "You know we can get fuckin brutal if needed. Just do your thing and know we're right beside you."

I don't want to waste any more of this day thinking about this fucker, so I lead the guys out the door.

We all take our own trucks and the sounds of roaring engines soon rattle his fucking windows as we park all over the parking lot to his shop. *Wicked Ink* is on the door and I can see a chick with a buzz cut looking at us as we walk up.

The guys follow closely as I open the door and pass by the front desk. I open every fucking door in the place until I find him. He almost shits himself when we all enter the tiny room.

The young client of his moves quickly and we all step aside, letting her pass. She needs to get the fuck out of here anyway. "Go to K'Inked and ask for Karma, she'll fix up that shitty tattoo for you." I hear Luca stop the girl and I love what he says.

"Call the police, Vicki." He scrambles and yells over my shoulder. I see Nash take the phone from her, but can't hear what he says as she backs away.

I meet him against the wall and put my forearm on his throat. He chooses not to fight me, but I can see hate on his face. "What kind of piece of shit hits a woman?" He looks around the room frantically, only to find these guys wouldn't piss on him if he were on fire.

"This is my final warning. You're gonna stay the fuck away from Karma or I'll be back and I promise you won't have to worry about using that dick of yours again." I hear shit crashing behind me, but don't dare take my eyes off of him.

"Do you fucking hear me?" I shove against him harder and wait for him to gasp out some sort of yes before I grip him by the shirt and toss him onto the floor. I look over my shoulder and see Luca, Levi, and Rome tearing the place up while Nash and Knox glare at the piece of shit at their feet.

Nash adjusts his cowboy hat before he lifts him to his feet. He only continues to torment the asshole. "Do you know what happened to the last mother fucker I saw hit a woman?" He waits for Ryan to shake his head no, before he responds. "He had to go to the fuckin' hospital to have a pitchfork removed from inside his ass. Think about that when you raise a hand and know we're watching. If you so much as slap one on the ass during sex, we'll know." He squeezes Nash's arm as he pushes even harder.

Luca yells for Rome to move out and we all follow. We're near the truck before I bust out laughing at Nash. "Dude. A fuckin' pitchfork? You made my ass clench thinking about that."

He smiles as he steps up into his truck. "Nah. I've said it many times though. Seems to get my point across quite nicely."

"No shit!" Levi yells out before we all take off again.

I add security to Karma's house and shop on the way back to the Alpha House. I also call in a favor with one of our bouncers at *Club Royal* to see if he can dig up any dirt on Ryan and maybe get him taken in. He's a filthy guy and I can only imagine the shit he's done.

Karma still hasn't called or texted and even though I've wanted to reach out to her, I haven't. I have an hour to get cleaned up before our live show tonight, so I move quickly through the house and don't waste any time hitting the shower.

Just knowing I'm about to see her excites me, even though I have no intentions of pushing anything with her.

Before I can even step out of the shower, Alpha is busting in and standing on the wet shower floor, licking anything he can get to. "Shit, boy. Do you need water in your bowl?" He looks at me with his bulldog resting bitch face and I have to laugh at him. "Karma is about to be here. You need to work your damn magic with her. Put in a good word for me." He walks slowly behind me as I continue to talk to him through the house.

"What the fuck? Do you ever wear clothes?" Lynx walks through the back doors and starts in on me instantly. I look down at my towel and tug it loose, letting it hit the floor.

"Is this better?"

"Ah damn it, Blaze. Rebel is here and will be looking for me soon. Cover that fucker up." My laughter echoes through the house as I wrap the towel around me once again.

"Karma is coming soon, you ready for tonight's show?"

"Sure. I'm always ready for a show. Hell, just strap a camera to my dick and we'll do an all day show."

"You'd love that shit. Finally, one of your ideas I can veto because I know it'll be a disaster." He sits on the bar stool and leans his elbows on the countertop. I can see stress in his face, and I'm not sure whether I should ask him about it, or just let him be.

"You ok? Thought you had enough of this fucking place. I can always give you some stand by calls tonight."

"Fuck off with that nonsense. I'll be out of here as soon as I can. Rebel came by to give Envy a few things.

"How's the committed life?" I have to ask because he looks anxious about something.

"Best thing I ever did. Rebel is my life and I couldn't be happier."

His instant smile makes me jealous. It would be nice to be there one day; who knows maybe Karma and I will get there eventually.

I hear the sound of female voices coming toward the kitchen, so I don't respond.

Rebel, Envy, and Karma walk in and I catch Karma looking at me the second she steps through the door.

She actually walks over to me and wraps her arms around me with a giant smile on her face. "Thank you boys for helping me get some talent in my shop. I feel like I can breathe a little." She turns to Lynx right after she hugs me. She doesn't give him the same up close treatment, but I do get to watch her ass as she talks to him.

She's obviously dressed to kill for the show and fuck my life if she didn't succeed in making me crazy. Her ass cheeks are barely covered in her short shorts and her tits are on display in a tight, low cut t-shirt.

Lynx and the other two girls walk out of the kitchen and she starts to follow them before I grab her hand to stall her.

"Why are you in a towel?" Her eyes graze over my body and there's only one thing to do at this point. I drop the towel again and see surprise wash over her face. My dick springs to action and I stand there and let her take me in. "Blaze, what the hell? Someone will see you."

"They're used to seeing me walk around naked, pretty sure this is nothing new to all the guys in this house."

She reaches for the towel and wraps it around my waist. I

smile at her attempt to do it without bumping into me.

"Ok. Cover up. This isn't for the world to see. If you want to do something like this, do it in your bedroom."

"Does that mean you'll be in my room, because if not it'll just be me and my dick in an empty room. Can't say it has the same effect."

She starts laughing and I can see Karma is finally here in a playful mood and it looks like this night is going to go well if this is any indication.

"I would, but we'd be late for the show." I take the towel from her and purposely give her another peek at me, and she doesn't miss the chance to look.

"Next time you have to give the show. I'll pull the towel from you instead of covering you though."

"Will you be wearing underwear at least for the show? I'm thinking it might go over better."

"Nope. I'll be laying on my stomach most of the time and besides, that part of my tattoo will go over my left ass cheek."

I can see approval on her face the second I express my thoughts on the ink I want. "I'd like some sort of demon on my leg and then have that tied in to a few objects I have in mind. It'll be a few sessions for what I'm wanting and I'm willing to give the live show the first one, but for the rest I expect us both to be naked."

"Oh really? You really think its sanitary and normal for me to tattoo you while I'm freaking naked?"

"Don't want it to be normal. I want to be the one and only to have you that way. It'll make me rare and this is what I strive to be."

She smiles and starts to walk out of the room. We've now fallen way behind the others, but that was my plan.

"Alright, let's get in there and get this show started. We're wasting valuable time where I could be working on you."

I follow without another word and just appreciate the view.

We open the door and Envy is already set up and it finally slaps me in the face that she's one of my potential prospects for the house. I think I'll have to watch and see how she handles the crowd tonight and really think on this. Her body is smokin' fucking hot, so that won't be an issue.

It doesn't take long for us to go live and I purposely sit back and let Karma do the intro to her show. She's saying a few things, but I'm not even listening to her. She tied her shirt tightly behind her back and now I can see every single curve of her body and that does nothing but grab all of my attention.

"Alright, Playboy. It's time to get you strapped down to this table so I can have my way with you."

She smiles at me with her challenge and I move willingly. I mean, who am I to argue about letting her have her way with me? Sign me up right fucking now.

"Looks like we'll be starting a leg piece for Blaze today and it's a privilege to get the honor to do this for him. I mean after all, I know my work will be seen by millions of callers and fans of his and this is kind of a big moment for me." She hands me the monitor as she continues to talk to the viewers.

"Blaze will be answering your questions tonight while I work on him. So please, don't hold back."

The first three questions come in about how hot the two women are and all of them are asking for them to have less clothes on. Well, that verifies that a female will be a great addition to the house and that it appears that Envy is a hot topic. I'll just ignore Karma being mentioned and stay level for this.

"As you all know, it takes time to do a quality piece. So make sure you're working with an artist who has the talent to pull off what you're wanting." She brushes her hand across my ass before she pinches it, secretly getting one in on me that I'll have to repay later.

I love seeing her like this. It seems like something has changed for her and I don't even want to ask what. I just want to enjoy it in case it's short lived.

She begins to draw on me and I know I have to remain very still, so I hand the monitor over to Envy. She takes over and begins working the viewers better than I expected her to. Her knowledge of the equipment Karma is using partnered with that smile of hers is raking in the attention. Honestly, she's getting more back and forth questions with the viewers than I am.

About an hour passes by and Karma has been working relentlessly, all the while entertaining the viewers with Envy. I'm simply a piece of art in this show and it makes me proud of both of them.

I think we've really got something solid to add to the house and it's only going to get better. I'll have to see if Envy is interested in becoming a full timer in here. I'd hope she'd not be able to turn down the money I can offer her.

"Looks like time is up. I'll keep working on this and I'll be sure and show the finished piece off in a future show. Make sure you tune in next week; looks like I have a couple who want matching tattoos and of course, I talked them into each getting a very special piercing."

Envy pulls the camera away from Karma and finishes the closing of the show like a pro.

"That was amazing. I had so much fun," Envy says with a grin.

Karma acts surprised by how much she liked it. "You did great! I'll have to make sure you're here with me each week!"

I don't mention my plans for Envy yet. I still need to do some thinking and planning of house rules before I can execute something like that.

"Envy. You can head out. I'm just going to work on this a bit." Karma's eyes meet mine and a rush of warmth flows over my body. I can anticipate where this is going and I can't fucking wait.

Envy leaves with very little encouragement and Karma follows her to lock the door. I watch her pull off her top and bra, before she slides her shorts off, proving that she's not wearing any panties.

"Fuck me. I've been waiting on this. Make sure you brush those titties over my back when you lean over me." My laughter is a mix of excitement and a tease toward her. She moves to me and slides her fingers down my body, before she straddles my back. I can feel her naked body around me and it sucks that I can't roll over and dive in.

"You're a fuckin' tease."

"You'd better get used to it. I plan to do this every damn day." I freeze with her words. Is she saying what I'm thinking she's saying?

"Are you fucking with me?" I'm practically twisting my body around to get a glimpse of her reaction.

"No. What you said to me last night really got to me. I think I can try this if you promise to keep a level head about my career and what I have to do to grow my business." I lean back down on the table and relax to let her continue working on me.

"That I can handle. I told you, this should be a happy time for you. You have me to relieve any stress you have and things can only get better from here with your shop."

"I hope you're right. Like I said I'll give it a true shot with you, but with my condition." I can easily agree to that, in fact it'll help me work with her on what I do and how I'll need even more understanding than what she's asking for.

"As long as I can keep you in my arms at night, I'm sure the rest will work itself out."

"Good, because that's where I plan to be every night. Just think . . . I can tattoo you all the time. My titties on display for you and you can't move a muscle."

"I can move. I'll end up with some fucked up tattoos, but I'll be able to move."

"I look forward to all of it with you." I can feel the gun going faster as she tries to finish up my piece. A feeling of relief takes me into an almost slumber as I relax and think about all the good things going on for me right now.

I hope she plans to stay the night tonight, because if she is, I'm about to be the happiest mother fucker in this house.

Chapter
TWENTY NINE

Karma

Two Weeks Later . . .

BLAZE AND I HAVEN'T LEFT his bed all damn day and a part of me really doesn't want to. Being here with him has proven to be peace and comfort for me. Not to mention extremely sexually satisfying.

I don't know how Blaze has as much energy as he does, but I hope he never loses it, because I'm living every girl's dream right now.

Wrapping one hand in Blaze's hair, I yank it to the side and slowly ride him, while tattooing a small heart on his shoulder.

"Hold still unless you want me to fuck this up," I tease.

"You know I can't hold still when your pussy is wrapped around my cock. Plus, I still want to see how good you can tattoo me through that orgasm I promised."

I pull the gun away from his skin and close my eyes, letting out a small moan as he bounces me off his lap a few times, before pushing me down onto him with all his strength.

"Shit, Blaze. You sure you want to test this?"

"Fuck, yes," he whispers against my ear. "If you mess it up then I'll always have the memory of why. My dick buried deep inside your pussy, claiming you."

I laugh against his neck and then reach over to dip the tip of the gun back into the ink. "Shit, Blaze. The things you talk me into."

He smiles that fucking smile that melts my damn heart and then buries his hands into my hair as I begin tattooing him again.

I begin to moan and bite my bottom lip, trying hard to concentrate as Blaze carefully moves inside of me, hitting just the right spot.

"Fuck yes. Keep going, baby," he moans out. "I want my cum in you before you finish this shit."

His movements pick up, causing my lines to become shaky, but he doesn't seem to care. "Keep going," he demands.

I dip the gun back into the ink and continue, while moaning out from his movements.

"Blaze . . . shit . . ." My orgasm rocks through me, causing me to lose the tattoo gun and grip onto Blaze's hair for support.

As soon as I yank his hair, he releases his load inside me, burying himself as deep inside as he can, while he bites my neck. "Holy fuck . . . You done with my tattoo?"

I look down at his slightly fucked up heart tattoo and laugh. It's small enough that it won't stand out too much. "Yup. Every time you look in the mirror you'll be reminded of me now. Congratulations."

He lifts a brow in amusement, and then turns me over onto my back and slowly trails kisses up and down my body.

"I want you in my bed every night and every fucking morning when I wake up. No more running from me, Karma."

I kiss the top of his head and laugh. "I've been in your bed every night and every morning for over two weeks now. I'm gonna have to sleep in my bed again at some point."

"Then I'll sleep in it with you," he says against my stomach, before kissing it. "We should get ready for the cookout."

I wrap my legs around his head and laugh when he starts kissing me and teasing me. "We don't have time for that, Blaze."

"Fuck . . . we'll make time."

Laughing, I put my foot on his shoulder and push him back. "I'm taking a quick shower." I quickly clean up his tattoo and then run away to the shower, before Blaze can try to talk me out of it.

I hear one of the guys yell at him to hurry his ass up and get downstairs to help man the grill, right as he's about to jump in the shower with me.

"Fucking, Rome. Looks like what I want to do to you will have to wait until tonight."

Blaze jumps under the water and quickly cleans up, before crushing his lips to mine and then leaving me alone to finish up.

My chest instantly aches to be near him the second he leaves, which is only further proof that I've completely fallen for him.

Each and every day he finds another way to crawl his way under my skin. There's no denying my feelings for him at this point, so there's no point in even trying.

I've completely given in to him and I don't regret it for one fucking second.

An hour into the cookout, everyone is having a great time hanging by the pool, drinking and eating leftovers.

The girls are chillin' by the water, talking about Netflix while the guys are playing basketball in the pool, roughing each other up.

Rebel invited one of her friends into the Alpha House for the first time and I swear I've never seen a girl so damn excited in my life.

Remi sits up and winks at Rome when he looks her way and pushes his way out of the pool. "Holy fuck. I want to bite that man's fine ass."

Rebel shakes her head and laughs. "And I'm sure he'd let you too."

Blaze's eyes lock on me from the pool and I know with that one look that he's counting down the minutes until he can get me alone again.

He grins at me and then tackles Luca under the water, stealing the ball from him.

I'm not gonna lie . . . it's hot as hell watching these boys get rough with each other.

Blaze

I LOVE HAVING HER HERE at the house and knowing that she isn't going to run every damn time I turn my eyes away.

The past two weeks have been perfect and we've actually managed to function properly in our careers even with the heavy sexual attraction we no longer hold back on. She's dick crazy for sure, but that's ok, I'm pussy crazy for her. Titties crazy. Ass crazy. Crazy about her tattoos. Crazy about her personality. Hell, just fuckin' crazy when it comes to her all together.

What can I say, she does it for me.

"Ah shit, Blaze has that look. He's about to tear up some pussy." Luca says it just loud enough that the guys in the pool can hear him, but not everyone else that's here.

"Not even gonna hide it, brother. Can't keep my hands off of her." I've never tried to hide my attraction to her. There's never been a reason to try.

"Can you please try to take it home a little sooner tonight? I mean shit, her moans all night long keep my dick hard and it's fucking annoying trying to talk myself down." Luca continues to push at me and I can't even get frustrated with him. She does moan all night most nights.

"Maybe you should sleep with the TV on or headphones in, because even if I take it home early, my dick will bounce right back when I pull her next to me."

"Alright, alright. Quit your damn bragging. You're lucky I let you have her." Rome moves closer and I let his shit roll off too.

"You didn't have a chance in hell after she held my dick. I'm telling you, it's magical."

They all bust up laughing and it forces a smile to know things can be normal in the house with her in my life. She and I understand what it's like to have a demanding career and work late almost every night. I've just shifted my schedule to be similar to hers and we end up sleeping late in the morning to make up for the late nights.

It's been a little strange doing the calls the more we bond, but I've managed to work out a way to get through them. Sex tapes of her riding me and just simply being her playful self keep me loaded for my callers.

I don't expect to do that part forever, but for now I have to keep things moving for business. The other guys can't handle all of the calls; in fact, it's about time to grow the house again.

I start to walk out of the pool and press down once more on the tape over my newest tattoo. I've been on a little binge when it comes to her inking me, but who could blame me? Today's was the first one she's done while I fucked her. She wants it to all look professional and I get that. Honestly, the heart is perfectly rough and will fit in well with the plan I have for my chest and shoulders.

I know I have an audience, and for that I'll grace them with only a partial show. She sees me walking toward her, standing there in her bikini and a partial cover up. Her smile widens as I get closer, but the look of fear takes over when she looks into my face.

"Blaze stop. We're in public. I know that look." I don't give her time to think about anything else before I've lifted her onto my shoulder and started my way into the house.

"Bye, fuckers. Next time don't interrupt me in the morning." Their laughter only gets louder as I walk us inside. She isn't even fighting me like she has in the past.

"Blaze. If you would've just said hey let's fuck, I would've followed you."

"Yeah, but this is more fun." She grabs my ass with her hands, so I return the favor with a slap to hers, causing her to scream out.

"I'd rather ride around your waist. But put me down before you take the stairs."

I don't listen to her as I take the stairs two at a time and get us to my bed. I slide her down the front of my body and her hands go straight to my beard before she slides them down my chest. "You're so impossible, but I love that about you. You didn't give up on me when I was pushing you away."

"I knew you'd be back. We just fit." I pull the strings to her bathing suit loose and watch her face while they fall to her feet. "You're so fucking sexy, Karma."

"You're not so bad yourself you know. A girl could really get used to rubbing her hands over all this." She spreads her hands over my shoulders and down my back.

"Run those nails over my back and all this talking is over. I'll fuck you so damn hard, you'll feel me on Monday." She smiles as she spreads her fingers and scrapes my back slowly, pulling the intensity out of me.

Fuck me. This girl is exactly what I needed. She matches me in every way and I can't wait to see where we go from here. There are so many possibilities and any other time I'd be able to see them all clearly, but right now I'm blinded by the thoughts of what I'm about to do to her.

"Get on your fucking knees on that bed and be ready for me take that pussy of yours." She teases me the entire way into position and I take my time working my way to her. Teasing is a little game we both play very well.

Fuck . . . we truly were made for each other.

COMING SOON~Book 3 in the Alphachat.com Series

To receive a text on release day text 'PLAY' to 213-802-5257

Or sign up for both of the author's newsletters which can be found on their websites!

About the Authors

Victoria Ashley

VICTORIA ASHLEY GREW UP IN Rockford, IL and has had a passion for reading for as long as she can remember. After finding a reading app where it allowed readers to upload their own stories, she gave it a shot and writing became her passion.

She lives for a good romance book with tattooed bad boys that are just highly misunderstood and is not afraid to be caught crying during a good read. When she's not reading or writing about bad boys, you can find her watching her favorite shows such as Supernatural, Sons Of Anarchy and The Walking Dead.

She is the author of Wake Up Call, This Regret, Slade, Hemy, Cale, Stone, Get Off On The Pain, Something For The Pain, Thrust, Royal Savage and is currently working on more works for 2016.

Contact her at:
Website: _www.victoriaashleyauthor.com_
Facebook: _www.facebook.com/VictoriaAshleyAuthor_
Twitter: @VictoriaAauthor
Intstagram: VictoriaAshley.Author

Books by

VICTORIA ASHLEY

WAKE UP CALL

THIS REGRET

SLADE (WALK OF SHAME #1)
HEMY (WALK OF SHAME #2)
CALE (WALK OF SHAME #3)

STONE (WALK OF SHAME 2ND GENERATION #1)

THRUST

GET OFF ON THE PAIN
SOMETHING FOR THE PAIN

ROYAL SAVAGE (SAVAGE & INK #1)

Hilary Storm

HILARY STORM LIVES WITH HER high school sweetheart and three children in Oklahoma. She drives her husband crazy talking about book characters everyday like they are real people. She graduated from Southwestern Oklahoma State University with an MBA in Accounting. Her passions include being a mom, writing, reading, photography, music, mocha coffee, and spending time with friends and family. She is a USA Today best-selling author of the Rebel Walking Series, Bryant Brother's Series, Inked Brother's Series, Six, and a co-author in the Elite Forces Series.

Contact her at:
Webpage: _www.hilarystormwrites.com_
Social Links
Facebook: _www.facebook.com/pages/Hilary-Storm-Author_
Twitter: @hilary_storm
Goodreads: _www.goodreads.com_

Books by

HILARY STORM

Six (Blade and Tori's story)
Seven (Coming Soon)

Rebel Walking Series
In A Heartbeat
Heaven Sent
Banded Together
No Strings Attached
Hold Me Closer
Fighting the Odds
Never Say Goodbye
Whiskey Dreams

Bryant Brothers Series
Don't Close Your Eyes

Elite Forces Series
ICE
FIRE
STONE (Coming in September

ACKNOWLEDGMENTS

Victoria Ashley

FIRST AND FOREMOST, I'D LIKE to say a HUGE thank you to Hilary Storm for taking a chance and writing this amazing story with me. It's my first time co-writing a book and I couldn't be more excited to have Hil with me on this journey. It's been quite a ride and I look forward to teaming up again to bring you some more sexy Alphas.

I'd also like to thank the beta readers that took the time to read our series: SE, Amy, Keeana, Lindsey and Amanda. We appreciate you ladies so much!

Kellie Montgomery for doing a wonderful job at editing and Dana Leah for her amazing design work on our cover.

And I want to say a big thank you to all of my loyal readers that have given me support over the last couple of years and have encouraged me to continue with my writing. Your words have all inspired me to do what I enjoy and love. Each and every one of you mean a lot to me and I wouldn't be where I am if it weren't for your support and kind words.

Last but not least, I'd like to thank all of the wonderful book bloggers that have taken the time to support our book and help spread the word. You all do so much for us authors and it is greatly appreciated. I have met so many friends on the way and you guys are never forgotten. You guys rock. Thank you!

ACKNOWLEDGMENTS

Hilary Storm

WOW WHAT A FUN RIDE this has been! I have to give a huge thanks to Victoria for wanting to write with me! I've always loved her writing and it was a great experience working alongside her for this book! Nothing like building from the heat we both already write on our own! It's been a great time and I can't wait until the next in the series!

My husband and kids are my life. Without their love and support I could never do any of this. It is through them that I have learned to love, live, and take chances. My heart is full because of these four and this book is no exception to that!

Betas Amanda and Lindsey . . . Thank you for always being so honest when you read my works! It means the world to me to know what you think!

Kellie- Thanks for cleaning it up for us! I love ya girl and I'm happy to have you in on this one!

Our loyal followers who will love this and share it like crazy, just like they always do. AND to the bloggers who support the author community . . . It is because of you that we keep writing with the urgency we do. We can't wait to share our stories with you so we can see how you react. Thank you for always allowing us to be a part of your lives through our words.

And last but definitely not least... I have to thank Dylan for making this cover amazing and giving me the inspiration for some of Blaze's shenanigans! It's been an amazing adventure so far working with you and I can't wait to see where this journey takes us!

Made in the USA
Middletown, DE
09 May 2019